Sheriff Warren Roberts

Sheriff Warren Roberts

- Sometimes The Only Choices -

S.A. George

iUniverse, Inc.
Bloomington

SHERIFF WARREN ROBERTS
SOMETIMES THE ONLY CHOICES

iUniverse books may be ordered through booksellers or by contacting:

iUniverse
1663 Liberty Drive
Bloomington, IN 47403
www.iuniverse.com
1-800-Authors (1-800-288-4677)

ISBN: 978-1-4620-4348-4 (sc)
ISBN: 978-1-4620-4349-1 (ebk)

Printed in the United States of America

iUniverse rev. date: 09/12/2011

TABLE OF CONTENTS

DEDICATION

To Ida and Rodger—Special People—Thank you always for encouragement and believing in what is possible.

To the Peace Officers who daily put their lives on the line—Thank you.

To the one who gives us inspiration and the spirit of survival, helping us to endure the greatest of obstacles and make a New Beginning.

To Kay—thank you for the encouragement and the typing.

EPIGRAPH

Sheriff Warren Roberts, who is called "extremely lucky", is led through the most challenging adventures of his career. He proves time and time again that he is an ally for those who need him and a formidable force to be reckoned with for those breaking the law. His encounter with a ghost has him searching for a murderer while trying to save lives at the Mansion. The words in the title "Sometimes the Only Choices . . ." refer to the only choices we might have in life as being bad ones, which is the Sheriff's dilemma dealing with bad circumstances he encounters.

Venezuela
Guyana
Suriname
French Guiana
Colombia
Ecuador
Peru
Brazil
Bolivia
Paraguay
Chile
Argentina
Uruguay

Venezuela
Guyana
Suriname
French Guiana
Colombia
Ecuador
Peru
Brazil
Bolivia
Chile
Argentina
Uruguay

CHARACTERS

1. Giles Macfarland: 85-year old British Philanthropist, Scientist, Doctor. Surrogate father to Max Fogel.
2. Max Fogel: German immigrant, son and assistant to Mr. Giles. Given stem cells to fight a disease. Had amassed a great deal of knowledge in the medical and scientific fields from being taught and doing research with Mr. Giles for twenty years, also head household attendant.
3. Marilyn Grant Macfarland: Love interest to Sheriff Warren Roberts. Married Giles Macfarland, girlfriend to Dante Stephens, Museum Assistant Curator in Houston.
4. Dante Stephens: Playboy, owned a demolition company, boyfriend to Marilyn Macfarland.
5. Sheriff Warren Roberts: Sheriff of the High Crimes Bureau in Houston. Romantically linked to Marilyn Grant. Invited to reading of will for Giles Macfarland and to find his murderer.
6. Louie Lamour Zimmerman: Dancer, actor, gay activist.
7. Father Benjamin: Priest where Mr. Giles attended church.
8. Tess Donner: Business woman, voice of an opera singer.
9. Patricia Fields: Real Estate Agent, part-time medium, claimed to conjure up spirits.
10. Angie Chang: Violinist, had dated Mr. Giles
11. Jason Jackson: Put away by Sheriff for murder, got early parole. Radio communications.
12. Palmer Sparrow: IRS employee, former bank CEO.
13. Bradley Johns: Computer geek, security systems.
14. Daniel Fashad: Doctor from India. Surgeon, knew Mr. Giles.

15. Rupert Schmitt: Friend of Max Fogel. Helped Max with research concerning Mr. Giles' Parkinsons and earlier when Max contracted tuberculosis, both emigrated from Germany.
16. Sylvia Diaz: One of the staff hired by Max who became his love interest.
17. Veronica: Sister to Marilyn Grant
18. Hector Flores: Cousin of Silvia Diaz
19. Raoul Diaz: Silvia Diaz's brother
20. Ramirez Diaz: Silvia Diaz's brother
21. Mr. & Mrs. Diaz: Silvia Diaz's parents
22. Giles Fairlane: Giles Macfarland
23. Mrs. Bradley: Head of staff after Max
24. Renee Benoit Klauss: Museum Curator in Brussels
25. Senator Marsdon: Senator from Texas, veteran
26. Nicole Matthews: Hector Flores' love interest, nurse
27. Dr. Bolviar: Head of group in Bolivia, Doctors Without Borders
28. Niah: Commander of Militia in Bolivia
29. Colonel Bennett: Friend of Sheriff Warren, in command of Special Ops
30. Lieutenant Dawson: Worked for Sheriff Warren
31. Captain Bill Moseley: Worked at High Crimes Bureau in Houston
32. Luke Moseley: Son of Captain Moseley
33. Milo Jones: Gay activist friend of Louie Lamour Zimmerman
34. Little Giles: Son of Silvia and Max Fogel
35. Flora: Daughter of Silvia and Max Fogel
36. Captain Rita Ruiz: Captain in Niah's Militia
37. Matthew Gray: Son of Rupert and Sarah
38. Alex Mayfield: An operative working for Sheriff Warren
39. Angie: Assistant to Rupert Schmitt
40. Daniella: Collaborated with Dante Stephens in covert activities and art theft
41. Holt: Collaborated with Dante Stephens
42. Shay: Collaborated with Dante Stephens
43. Winston: Museum Art Curator, collaborated with Dante Stephens
44. Chief Constable Williams: Worked at Scotland Yard
45. Lieutenant Wayne: Worked for Chief Constable Williams
46. Dr. Rhodes: Lead scientist conducting convention at Oxford University

47. Guardians of the Flower: In Bolivian jungle they guard a sacred mountain producing flowers having a healing property.
48. The General: Serves to protect Niah, was a Guardian
49. Dr. Isidro: Oncologist, scientist, friend of Mr. Giles
50. The Big Guys: Prisoners who helped Sheriff Warren and the 'Camp' residents fight the Cartel
51. Markus Berber: Art collector, friend of Marilyn
52. Agent Scott: Worked for Chief Constable Williams
53. Remmy: A Russian dealing with the black market

CHAPTER 1

Beginnings

2010

Austin, Texas

Sheriff Warren Roberts had been working in Austin for ten years. Twenty people worked under him. Crime was down. That day he had been parked at a large convenience store studying the traffic flow when suddenly a woman sped past him in a sports car. He followed her, finally pulled beside her, siren on.

"Pull over," he motioned as he said it.

She did so. The Sheriff got out of his car, he was tall and slender, auburn colored short hair, moustache and goatee.

She rolled down her window. "Ma'am, I need to see your license and registration."

"I'm Marilyn Grant and my license and registration are at my house." She was about 5'6", petite, medium brown shoulder length hair today worn in a French twist.

"You ran a stop sign, going sixty in a forty."

"Please, can't you just . . . I could . . ."

"Offering me a bribe Ma'am?"

"Certainly not. Follow me to my house and I'll find both."

The Sheriff thought for a moment, "All right."

When they got there she produced her license and registration. "And I would like to offer you a bribe," she said in a sexy voice.

She walked him to her bedroom and then . . .

An hour later, "We definitely need to talk Darlin'," he said.

"One more kiss," she said as many times before when they acted out this charade.

"Marry me," he said to her over dinner. "I'm taking a job offered to me as Sheriff with Houston's High Crimes Bureau. Police, Sheriff's departments working together, starting $80,000."

Marilyn looked at him, "Still dangerous."

"Crossing the street is dangerous," he laughed. He hesitated for a moment then, "We've been at this crossroads now for two years, known each other forever . . . do you love me?"

"Yes, I love you."

"Something is different, what is it?"

She stood up, "I'm not big on commitments."

"You're not kidding."

"You do all these impressive things, two degrees from Stanford."

"You have the museum, working on a doctorate in art, the exhibits, what are you getting at?"

"I can't settle down with someone in a dangerous job who might never come home." She was serious about the dangers in his line of work.

"Any excuse will do?" Warren was puzzled. "If you've met someone, have the courage to be honest with me."

"Plans change Warren, my plans have changed."

"Then there's no reason to keep hoping?" He got up, dressed, "Let me know how you're doing, I'll be at the Bureau." He kissed her bye and left.

She loved him but the security of a much older wealthy husband, a philanthropist appealed to her needs more than her love for Warren.

A month later she became Mrs. Giles Macfarland. Warren knew about the wedding but didn't attend.

A year passed.

["Giles Macfarland, Houston Philanthropist dies under mysterious circumstances. The funeral will be held at the Macfarland mansion."] a news report said. Warren wondered about Marilyn, had she gotten what she wanted and found happiness?

CHAPTER 11

Giles' Funeral Planned

Marilyn began planning her deceased husband's funeral along with Max Fogel who had known him for twenty years. Marilyn's eyes were swollen from crying, he comforted her.

"I loved him," she said.

"He knew that Miss." Max sat with her in the smaller kitchen, the mansion had three.

"We'll get through this, although I don't know how . . . and you are like a son to him. How are you holding up?"

"Not very well, I'm trying to keep it together."

"This is your house for as long as you want to stay."

"Dante wants me to go, I heard him."

"It's obvious he wants to make life miserable, I should have never done what I did when I was married to Giles."

"Put that behind you now." He sat facing her, took her hands in his as she cried. "He is an abuser, I could throttle that guy and he would never bother you again."

"Max don't, please, he's dangerous and capable of anything . . . it would only make things worse."

"You are bruised."

"I don't believe he murdered Giles," she said, "I can cover the bruises."

"Do you need him enough to put up with this?"

Suddenly Dante walked in. "Marilyn, Max, how are the arrangements going?" He asked this unmoved and uncaring.

"Slowly," Marilyn said.

Max started writing on his notepad anything pertinent to the funeral as he tried to ignore Dante. Dante then left for business in town.

"Excuse me Miss, I have calls to make, write down anything you need to discuss with me."

Max left. He felt a part of himself die that day; he mourned for Mr. Giles but kept his emotions in check for now.

CHAPTER III

Giles' Funeral

Two hundred attended the funeral held at the mansion, the mass for Christian Burial was given, and the Rosary was performed the night before in a church attended by Mr. Giles. Tess Donner, a friend, sang "I Dreamed a Dream", one of his favorites. Several spoke, many travelled great distances from several countries to be there. Max was the last to speak offering only praise for the man he had assisted for twenty years, never mentioning his status as Mr. Giles' son, or his own education and collaboration with him. Then he motioned for the casket to be closed. The white pall remained covering it. He took his seat again between Silvia Diaz, his love interest and Marilyn. They all held hands as another song was performed "Pieu Jesu." Marilyn, as she held hands with Max, knew he was struggling to hold up but was about to lose that battle. He attended the wake after the funeral.

A few hours later when the guests had left, Max loosened his tie and sat motionless in the parlor, eyes closed, exhausted.

Marilyn remarked how exceptional the funeral had been. "Are you going to be all right?"

"I will Miss, get some rest yourself."

Dante took her upstairs. Silvia came over to Max.

"You look beautiful," he told her, as he held her hand. "I don't want to be alone tonight, stay with me."

"I will," she said. "I'll meet you upstairs."

All night he sat crying quietly, he resisted sleep.

"How can I ease your pain?" she asked as she stroked his hair.

"Just stay with me."

Finally several hours later he slept.

The next day Silvia had breakfast with him in the kitchen, both had circles under their eyes, his were swollen. When no one was around he kissed her.

"You saw me through a very rough night, thank you pretty girl."

She kissed him as she began her chores.

"There are some business matters of Mr. Giles I must attend to then I'll be back to help."

The ladies tending to the activities in the mansion became very aware of Silvia's relationship with Max and gave her more than enough advice.

CHAPTER IV

A Week after the Funeral

A week had passed since the funeral. Max was sleeping restlessly by Silvia.

"Max", a voice whispered. He woke up. "Max, come downstairs."

He did without waking Silvia.

"Who are you?" He saw no one.

"Mr. Giles."

"That's not possible." Max was now in the vault area. "Where are you?"

"Here, beside you. You can't see me, open the vault."

Max did, something then moved past him into the body of Mr. Giles. Then Mr. Giles removed himself from the vault and walked toward him, Max stepped back.

"Missed you," he said and touched Max's face who was kept in an almost dream state. "Go back to bed, we'll talk tomorrow, this was only a dream."

Max entered his room upstairs again and slept.

The next day Silvia questioned him, "Where did you go?"

"I don't remember leaving. I had a dream about Mr. Giles," he told her. He was puzzled as was she especially when he noticed a large cut across his hand. Everyone got to work.

That evening as Max was doing research in the lab, Mr. Giles appeared behind him. Max turned to see him, he couldn't process this and turned back to his research refusing to believe that it was Mr. Giles.

"You aren't really here."

"Oh, but I am."

"Last evening?"

"You came to the vault and freed me."

Max faced him, "Then it wasn't a dream." This unnerved him.

"Can you handle this, seeing me again as I appear now?"

". . . It will take getting used to. How is this possible? How is it that I have you back?"

"I can't explain completely, not now. I am back and have a plan continuing our research and finding who murdered me."

"Then you were right, you had a feeling that you would be murdered. Don't make me forget what you have me do for you Mr. Giles," Max said emphatically.

"Only last night, no more."

"What about Marilyn? Dante continues to abuse her."

"I have looked in on her, unfortunately she has fallen prey to his charm and good looks, he's been spending too much time with her, I'll take care of it. Don't tell her about me, not yet. Your place is still here Max, even if Dante doesn't approve, don't leave. I saw the funeral, well done to both you and Marilyn. Now down to business. This is what I need you to do, the reading of the will is to be in three weeks."

Max was given a list of people to invite and also to contact a certain Sheriff Warren Roberts.

CHAPTER V

Reading of the Will—Ultimatum

A letter was delivered to Sheriff Warren three weeks after the funeral to attend the reading of the will and investigate the suspicious death of Giles Macfarland. Max, Mr. Macfarland's assistant delivered the letter personally. He was a tall young man, black shoulder length hair parted in the middle worn in a ponytail, clean shaven, large brown eyes, looked serious, his usual demeanor, physically fit, always wore black and suspenders, spoke with a German accent.

"Good to meet you Sheriff."

"Likewise Mr. Fogel."

"I have worked for Mr. Macfarland for twenty years, he wrote this letter days before he died requesting that you attend."

Warren read it. "He suspected someone of trying to murder him?"

"Yes Sheriff."

"And Mrs. Macfarland?"

"No threats have been made against her, the grieving widow had also requested your help."

"I'll be there."

"Tomorrow at 2:00 p.m."

The house was in an isolated area of Houston only reached taking one lane roads up a hill. Thirty thousand square feet, three stories, large basement, two huge iron gates prevented any uninvited from approaching. The house was literally a museum filled with artifacts from around the world, antiques, paintings, many were given as gifts to Mr. Macfarland over the years. Several guests had arrived, the gates allowed the last one inside, Sheriff Warren, and closed behind. Max welcomed him. Warren was dressed appropriately in a dark suit.

Marilyn came to the door and hugged him. "How handsome you look," she said, "glad you came."

Seeing Marilyn all the memories flooded in. "Are you holding up?" he asked.

"Barely, come with me."

Warren was impressed with the immense house and its elaborate furnishings.

Marilyn introduced him, "Everyone, this is Sheriff Warren Roberts, a friend attending to some business matters here." She didn't tell them the real reason for Warren being there, to keep order and solve a murder. He would question each guest and begin his investigation immediately after the reading.

All in attendance had known Giles Macfarland with the exception of Warren, Giles had been a father figure to Marilyn who was forty-five years younger than her eighty-four year old husband. She had a young lover on the side, Dante Stephens who could fulfill her other needs, they sat together.

"The will is about to be read by Mr. Macfarland's attorney," Max told them. Everyone was seated in front of a large plasma set where the attorney then had a two-way conference with the guests from his office in town.

"The Sheriff will keep order as the will is read," the attorney began. He mentioned every name listed in the will. "All of you will receive a gift of $100,000 each and a trinket from Mr. Macfarland. Marilyn Macfarland inherits everything, property, monies, stocks, furnishings." There were gasps and outbursts from some as Marilyn was named. "And Max Fogel inherits all monies from research, patents, grants, books written and afterward to his heirs if he is deceased; if no heirs then to the school Rice University." Neither Max nor Marilyn reflected any emotion over the designations in the will as they sat quietly. Dante now made plans to marry her as quickly as possible so he could move to control her inheritance.

Then the attorney mentions a DVD that Giles Macfarland had made to be played after the attorney's transmission ended.

"I don't know what it says but it is to be played immediately. Good-bye and good luck to you all."

Max and the Sheriff tried to keep the guests quiet. The DVD was played on the plasma.

["I Giles Macfarland have been murdered. You are each suspects. The Sheriff's true purpose here is to find who murdered me. I have known all of you in some capacity. Marilyn and I hosted a gala a month ago. That evening I became ill and fell into a coma and died three days later. The Sheriff will begin his investigation after lunch is served, no one will be allowed to leave here until the guilty one is named. As an added incentive, one of you will die every twenty-four hours. The Sheriff and my staff are not suspects, however, he will die along with all of you if the murderer isn't found."]

The Sheriff sat stone-faced for a few moments, he then quickly took charge. He and four others tried to force their way out the front doors. Max had tried to help them but concluded there was no way out, not even he knew that Mr. Giles had planned this.

"I didn't know he was capable of this," he told them.

"Mr. Macfarland is dead."

"He is here Sheriff, his spirit inhabits this house and it is he that is keeping all of us here."

"If I believed you, who would carry out the executions?"

"I suppose he will," Max replied.

"Are you able to communicate with him?"

"Yes."

"Is Marilyn a suspect?"

"Yes." Max knew better but was protecting her from others who might die."

"Max, I need your help," Warren said.

"You'll have it."

"I have a feeling that you're going to get the brunt of the fallout from this."

"Yes and so will you."

Warren looked at the others, "We need to examine the vault where Mr. Giles is buried."

Six agreed to come with him. Marilyn went as well. They reached the basement where the vaults were located, several of Giles Macfarland's family members were interred there. His vault was opened and to add to the fears of those watching no body was found. Marilyn started shaking as she listened carefully unable to believe that the ghost of Giles Macfarland was a reality.

"Does Mr. Giles appear to you Max?" Warren asked.

"Yes."

"A spirit inhabiting a dead body," Dante said sarcastically.

Max looked around at the others then at the Sheriff . . . "Yes".

There was quiet for a moment then, "Let's eat something," Bradley said, introducing himself to the others. "I'm the computer geek. I used to help Mr. Macfarland and Max with the computer and electronics problems as well as security . . . fantastic ghost story Max, I almost believed it."

A small man in round glasses, wearing a lavender jacket and matching fedora approached Max. "I'm Louie Lamour, can we get something to eat?"

"Certainly, let's go, the staff will fix something."

"Bring the wine." Louie requested all he could get.

That afternoon after they finished lunch, Warren asked to talk with the staff, the three women and Max who ran the household wouldn't be in danger as stated in the DVD made by Mr. Giles. The gardener and crew had left earlier along with two other staff before the reading began.

"But like yourselves we cannot leave until the case is solved," Max said. He then introduced Warren to Mrs. Bradley who was over the staff after himself, he had hired her six years earlier. "Mrs. Bradley, if you could take a few minutes, this is Sheriff Warren. I told him you know everything that goes on around here. Be as forthcoming as you need to be." He then left.

"Nice to meet you Ma'am. These questions concern Mr. Macfarland's murder. The gala and the funeral Mrs. Bradley, anything out of these events that could help us?"

"We respected Mr. Giles, we all called him that, not so formal, he is a ghost and we are being held here until this murder is solved."

"How do you know, have you seen him?"

"I only see what he can do. Each person here has something to atone for. Mr. Giles was a good man but everyone has enemies. I was trying not to eavesdrop as Miss Marilyn and Max began planning Mr. Giles' funeral here in this kitchen. Miss Marilyn's eyes were swollen from crying, she had bruises. She is no murderer. Dante Stephens is a very calloused individual who abuses her. I suspect him. He then seemed very uncaring about the plans for Mr. Giles' interment wounding both Miss Marilyn and Max further and wanting Max out of the house as soon as possible."

Warren became so angry with Dante, he already pegged him as guilty. "And the others?"

"The one called Patricia mentioned wanting a book belonging to Mr. Giles, a book on the occult. Not a murderer."

"Father Benjamin has a dark secret from the past and Mr. Giles was aware of it, perhaps a motive."

"Louie Lamour drinks too much and spills secrets. No motive."

"Tess Donner has been a fashionista with Mr. Giles' help, operatic voice . . . sang at the funeral, it's not her."

"Miss Chang, the violinist, dated Mr. Giles. No."

"Mr. Jackson you knew in the past, he didn't murder Mr. Giles but he did his family. I read about it when you testified against him." This startled Warren hearing her statement on the man.

"Palmer Sparrow was terrible to Mr. Giles but he wasn't the one—he enjoyed tormenting him as opposed to murder."

"Bradley made the house more secure, he's young, made mistakes, not a murderer."

"Dr. Fashad operated on Mr. Giles' late wife, pushed her up on the transplant list. Later she became pregnant, the transplant failed during the pregnancy, she and the baby died, she had miscarried before—was he to blame? I don't know. He didn't murder Mr. Giles."

"Some of these people out of 200 guests at the gala had found fault with Mr. Giles and vice versa but they respected him, all but the one."

"Thank you for your time," Warren said, amazed at her observation. Warren then made suggestions to the others. "Look for clues, anything that looks suspicious." He tried to acquaint himself with everyone there. "Our lives will depend on the help we give each other. We should probably stay together as much as possible."

"Who put you in charge?" Dante asked.

"If you disagree with my suggestions, let's hear yours."

Dante didn't pursue it.

"We need to check police records on everyone here, that would include me for matters of trust. Any dealings with Giles Macfarland need to come out now, including the reading of the will."

Angie Chang played a violin belonging to Mr. Giles. It seemed to calm nerves as well as the wine, a special vintage. Patricia Fields met with Warren and Marilyn and offered to contact Mr. Giles in a séance.

Warren spoke politely to her, "Not now, if he is communicating with Max, don't . . . assuming there is a ghost."

However she had her own agenda as Mrs. Bradley alluded to finding that special book on the Dark Arts given to Mr. Giles.

Marilyn took Warren upstairs to his assigned room; all the guests had already been assigned rooms.

"Dante is occupied playing bridge," Marilyn said as she followed Warren to the room and went inside. He removed his coat.

"How are things", he asked her.

"My husband has died, things were good, I did love him. He was like a father figure to me, protecting me, giving me anything."

"And Dante?"

"I kept Dante through our marriage, he could satisfy me where Giles couldn't. I think Giles suspected I had someone. Am I a suspect?"

Warren didn't answer. "Are you going to marry him?"

"I don't know he's young, intolerant sometimes. He owns a demolition company."

"Is he good to you Marilyn?"

"Most times he is."

This disturbed Warren. "Do you believe Max that Giles is here?"

"I don't know, sometimes I feel like he is."

He touched her face and kissed her. She closed the door. They rekindled the love they had before Warren left her.

A while later she went downstairs. Warren followed later to study the crime scene where Mr. Giles had most likely been attacked, although no one was exactly sure where the crime scene was, falling then into a coma, dying in a hospital three days later. Warren had no assistance coming so he used what he had, borrowing latex gloves placing anything suspicious in plastic bags, using the camera in his cell phone to document anything of importance, information continued to be the most valuable tool. The others were instructed to look for evidence.

Dante was sitting downstairs with a glass of wine. "Have you solved the case?" he asked sarcastically.

"Wishful thinking," Warren replied.

The other guests were talking, nervous that no one could leave and could possibly be murdered. Four had decided to walk through the large library with Marilyn who was glad to show it.

"Giles had a collection of rare books. Pick something to read," she said, "we may be here a while."

Warren asked Dante about his demolition company.

"You are still in love with Marilyn?" Dante asked him. The question was more of a statement and caught Warren off guard.

"I'll always love Marilyn as a friend and be concerned for her happiness."

"Do you play chess?" Dante asked.

"Badly."

"I graduated with honors from Harvard, a PHD in physics. Did you attend college?" intending to embarrass Warren.

"Actually I graduated from Stanford, masters degrees in forensic science and criminal and judicial law. 4. GPA."

"Impressive for . . ."

"For someone from the stix?"

By then several, including Max, were around listening to the conversation. Marilyn was there and heard it.

"Perhaps you both need a ruler to measure your egos," Tess said.

"Wine anyone?" Max asked.

"Beer?"

"Beer it is Sheriff."

Warren and Dante continued the chess game. He continued to ask Dante about his company.

"I grew up making things, bombs, explosives."

"How did you learn to make homemade bombs?"

"My dad didn't encourage this. What chemicals I needed were on the internet. Many of them were in our own backyard, so-to-speak. Fertilizer, timers, anything. I did end up for a time in Juvenile Hall because I blew up mailboxes. Got my life straightened out, inherited my father's demolition company after working there a few years. Then after a tour of duty in Iraq, I returned home knowing how to make virtually any IED and do what I do best, blow up things. I should tell you I text when I drive, arrest me . . . what's your story?"

"Afghanistan, guns, weaponry, my specialty was sharpshooter." Warren now knew Dante was a mental case capable of anything including murder, as they conversed his suspicions and dislike grew.

The chess game now ended.

"Checkmate," Dante said.

"You play well."

Warren saw Jason Jackson watching the game and him.

"Mr. Jackson."

"Sheriff."

Warren sat in a chair facing him.

"I was wondering when you'd get around to me, it didn't go well last time."

"No it didn't, not for murder."

"I was paroled, served ten years, ten long years, you convinced them I was guilty, circumstantial evidence."

"You got a second chance Jason, convince me you had nothing to do with Giles Macfarland's death. How did you know him?"

"Antennas, radio and satellite communications. Four weeks ago everyone here was part of a gala thrown by Mr. Giles and his wife. He fell into a coma that evening and was dead three days later according to his wife and the staff. I didn't kill the guy. He was a big fish. I made my living on the big ones."

"How are things since your parole?" Warren asked delicately.

"Hard to find a job when people think you murdered your family. I was lucky, I had skills going into prison and more when I left. Do you still believe I'm guilty?"

"It doesn't matter what I believe. Appreciate your time."

Warren left him. Bradley had collected what he thought might be evidence, handing a silver cuff link to Warren in a plastic bag.

"Marilyn Macfarland said it had belonged to her husband, there is a speck of blood on it."

"Thanks Bradley."

"Hope it helps."

Warren placed it a cabinet designated for evidence. He then borrowed a flashlight from Max and continued to look around. It was late. Marilyn found him, she was afraid. Warren calmed her. He wanted her again but restrained himself in favor of hunting down a killer. He sent her to the parlor for safety reasons, to be with the others who wouldn't go to their rooms that night staying together feeling more protected. Warren had written notes concerning the crime scene and those he had interviewed.

Around midnight Warren was awakened still in his suit, now a familiar sound from a gun prepared to fire. He quickly got up, "Who's there?" No answer. Suddenly three shots rang out, Warren fell, the intruder left. Soon after, Max who was very perceptive arrived and found Warren.

"Who did this Sheriff?"

Warren could barely talk as he was dying. "I never saw . . ."

Max didn't have a way to reach Mr. Giles as he used to by cell phone, so he began talking. "Mr. Giles, if you hear me the Sheriff is dying, three bullets pierced his abdomen."

Mr. Giles reached Max quickly giving Warren a shot in his neck.

"A paralyzing agent, he is technically dead but this agent should give us an hour to revive him before it's too late . . . have him taken to the vault." Giles left him.

Max stayed with Warren as the others came. Daniel felt for life signs then pronounced him dead. Marilyn had come quickly with Dante, she knelt by Warren crying. They wrapped him in blankets and moved him to the vault. They placed him on a bench and they talked for a few minutes. Max kept looking at his watch. Father Benjamin uttered a prayer. Dante glanced at Marilyn who was about to faint, he grabbed her and escorted her upstairs.

"Oh what now?" Louie asked nervously.

They then reluctantly left Warren. Everyone was affected by his death, seen as loosing the only help they had. There was a discussion held with Max.

"Giles Macfarland has us all trapped, are we next?" Tess asked.

Max took the brunt of their fears and anger.

"Are you doing this?" Father Benjamin demanded an answer.

"No," Max replied, "certainly not."

Marilyn stepped in front of Max to defend him. "I am as startled as you all are, my dead husband is sending threatening messages."

"I must leave for a while," Max said, "I'm not feeling well."

"I can handle it from here," she told him, "go rest."

The guests started insulting each other with accusations of being the murderer of Giles and now the Sheriff. Some drank themselves into a stupor. Some were now wearing night wear provided by Marilyn and the staff. Some separated themselves and went to their rooms, others remained playing chess or bridge. Television wasn't allowed by Mr. Giles.

Max retreated to the basement lab after he brought Warren from the vault. Giles had been setting up.

"I came as quickly as I could Mr. Giles."

"We haven't much time," Giles said.

A process was begun to bring Warren back.

"Three gun shots to the abdomen and he never saw his assailant?"

"No sir."

"We will soon see if the paralyzing agent worked."

Max quickly removed the bullets and sutured the wounds. They now discussed each step to save the Sheriff. Hours passed by as Giles and his protégé Max, whom he had taught for twenty years the sciences and medical field, began to bring Warren back. No one else knew about Max's background except Marilyn and those who knew about their research as certain schoolmates. Warren was submerged in a freezing mixture of chemicals, sonic bursts of energy and breathing an oxygen compound had begun to have the result they had hoped for.

"You are working tirelessly to bring him back," Mr. Giles remarked.

"I believe the Sheriff will find your answers and save their lives . . . you deceived them and me."

"That I did, I regret it but one of them is a murderer and I will exact my revenge."

Max realized that he couldn't stop Mr. Giles but still hoped he could reason with him.

Giles knew that Max was trying to adjust to all the changes, he wouldn't help Mr. Giles harm anyone. Another hour had passed.

"Sir, the flesh is turning a healthy color."

"Drain out the chemicals, remove him then to the heart lung machine."

"A blood transfusion will be needed," Max said, "who will provide it?"

"I believe Mr. Sparrow will be a willing donor once anesthetized, take these bags with you, no need to bring him here."

"Understood, O—from Mr. Sparrow."

Several hours would pass. Sheriff Warren was dressed again and placed on a sofa in another area of the large parlor, a note was given to Marilyn, she shrieked as she read it. ["You will need all the help you can get. I have brought the Sheriff back to you. The clock is ticking."]

It was early Tuesday morning. The others in the parlor found Warren asleep on a couch. Daniel examined him.

"He is alive, I don't know how. The bullets should have killed, did kill him."

"Wake him," another said.

Warren was disoriented and weak, then he saw Marilyn. She held his hand, he sat up, groaned in pain.

"What happened?" Marilyn asked.

". . . Don't remember."

Dante said, "You died."

"Do you remember anything? Who operated on you?" Daniel asked.

"No." He tried to stand up and saw the blood on his clothes. "Seems I need a wardrobe change."

"Take it easy," Daniel told him, "sit down." He examined the bullet wounds again. "Each one had fatal consequences."

Across the room they saw someone in a chair.

"It's Mr. Sparrow from Internal Revenue and it seems he has become severely anemic over the last few hours," Daniel observed.

Warren then realized that Palmer Sparrow had unwittingly provided him with a much needed blood transfusion. He stood up carefully.

"There is a blood donor card and a cashier's check for $100,000 in his pocket," Dante said.

"Giles said each one would receive a trinket and $100,000 for being here," Marilyn said, "but a donor card is ridiculous."

Louie mentioned, "There was a note about you Sheriff still helping us find the murderer."

"Just give me a few minutes," Warren said. "What about Mr. Sparrow?"

"We make him comfortable, he should make it." Daniel wasn't sure when he said this.

Dante looked at Warren then escorted Marilyn away. They all went for sandwiches, the staff had provided an early breakfast. Max looked after Warren.

"There are computers," Max told him, "at your disposal to compile information for research in the library. No calls, e-mail signals are blocked so no background checks, Mr. Giles' orders. Pain medicine is in your room, don't overexert yourself."

"Max, you should have been a doctor."

Warren was now aware of his new status as a modern day Lazarus. There were more stares and whispers.

"Some of you don't trust me now. If we don't unite in this we might all die. Either way I'm continuing the investigation. Cell phone cameras can document crime scenes. Any help will be welcome."

"I can help," Bradley said.

"We have to work on a way to free ourselves, some of you work on ideas."

"As what?" Dante asked, who had gotten a news clipping about his father's untimely death with a check for $100,000.

"You own a demolition company, homemade bombs ring a bell? Mr. Giles is sending all of us trinkets, reminders, we need to leave here soon."

"What about trying to send a signal from the roof?" Jason asked.

"Work it out." Warren had to rest before interviewing more people. "Back on the couch," he said.

Angie played a violin soft and soothing at first then came requests. She played for over an hour. There was singing and laughter for the moment.

Warren awakened, walked in to another room adjoining the parlor and talked to Bradley. "What did you do for Giles Mr. Johns?"

"Being a computer geek specialist, I can do several things. Specifically security systems. This was my job to help install a system at the Metropolitan Museum. Many of Mr. Macfarland's investments, paintings and art were there. There was a theft six months later, only could have been an inside job. My services were terminated. Mr. Macfarland lost a fortune, I didn't do it. I also installed security here."

"No one was accused? The investigation?"

"Went nowhere, so why was I invited here with the others? Oh and I received my check for $100,000 and a keypad used for security locks, should I think I'm next?"

"I think it means you'll live," Warren told him to alleviate his fear. He was sure Bradley hadn't killed anyone. "I don't know why you were invited with the rest of us, I'm certain Giles had his reasons."

Warren then talked to Angie Chang. "Miss Chang, may I have a few moments of your time?"

"Certainly Sheriff, or should I call you extremely lucky?"

"I am, there is obviously another doctor in the house. Daniel denies saving my life."

"We're facing termination for what? So a murderer won't go free?"

"That's about it."

"And you'll present this information to a ghost, Giles Macfarland?"

"Yes . . . by the way you play beautifully."

"Thank you, what do you want to ask me?"

"How did you know Giles?"

"I play a violin, as you know, that is my trade. Giles met me in China, I played there with the Beijing Symphony Orchestra. He encouraged me to move to America and play in the Houston Symphony. He was well connected, pulled strings, a bad pun, I admit, five years later I became first chair, concert master. We dated, I ended up going to New York to join the New York Philharmonic."

"Why New York?"

"I had met someone there who was in the symphony."

"It happens," Warren said remembering Marilyn's decision.

"Giles and I lost touch. I certainly wouldn't, didn't murder this generous man who helped my career, I loved him." She lifted her left hand showing Warren a bracelet. "If he is here, he gave me this beautiful bracelet and $100,000 . . . hope this is a good sign."

"Hope so too Miss Chang. Thank you for your time." Warren stood up. "Goodnight, I'm turning in," he said to whoever was listening. He felt he shouldn't sleep but weakness forced him to.

Later that night he dreamed of another victim, now not able to sleep he got up, went into the bathroom and was startled to see notes written on the toilet paper. He carefully unwound the roll tearing off the part that had been written on laying it on a desk in the bedroom. He turned on the light as he studied the writing from Giles. Confused he went back to the bathroom, where notes appeared again and then nothing more.

The next morning there was a commotion. Max knocked on Warren's door.

"Sheriff, one has died."

Warren opened the door, quickly dressed. Max knew he was still weak and in pain and assisted him.

"Who is it?"

"Mr. Sparrow."

Once downstairs Warren and Bradley used their cell phone cameras to document the death. Bradley took notes.

"Daniel, how did he die?" Warren asked.

"It appears he bled to death."

"No one heard anything," Tess said.

"Why aren't the police looking for us or the Sheriff's Department looking for you?" Father Benjamin asked.

"I don't have any way of knowing that."

"Maybe Mr. Macfarland has a way of changing what people perceive to be reality. Maybe nothing appears to be here," Louie suggested, "not the house, cars or us."

"Whatever made you come up with that idea?" Dante retorted.

"T.V., science fiction movies," he replied.

"He could be right," Patricia said. "We should have a séance."

Father Benjamin didn't like the idea.

"I need your assistance in the library for a few minutes, Max can you assist us?" Warren asked.

Soon they entered the library.

"I understand that Giles was into the Dark Arts."

"Perhaps he was," Max replied knowing that he was.

"Where would we find information about this?"

"There is a section of books over here." Max was uncomfortable with Warren's questions about Mr. Giles dealing with the occult. Father Benjamin began reading one of the books, as he did so, he felt a presence around him. Warren began reading another of those books in an attempt to understand what made Giles so powerful. Max found articles about each person there. "You might want to look at these," handing them to Warren. "One article is about you Sheriff."

"He's forcing us to face our fears before we die," Warren remarked.

"Or our worst moments," Father Benjamin replied.

Patricia entered the library. "One of Giles' books was left in my room with a check for $100,000, the book was on the occult . . . I might could help Sheriff."

Warren didn't ask her for a séance, instead he approached Father Benjamin. "Could you perform an exorcism?"

"Probably, if a person was possessed. Since Mr. Macfarland is believed to be a spirit I can do nothing but help find a way out of here."

"But I can," Patricia said.

"Read this." Warren handed her the articles inside a book of incantations. She read carefully.

"Apparently the dark magic has allowed him to survive in this house, he has become very strong but cannot leave."

"Unless he enters another body?"

"Right Sheriff, presumably the body of his murderer."

"Let's hope the murderer isn't a woman. What can we do to stop him?"

"At this point nothing."

"Appeal to him?"

"A séance. I can try an incantation as well. I don't understand why you were spared Sheriff, maybe you won't die."

"I died, I'll die again if we don't find the murderer."

Father Benjamin finished reading an article about himself involved in a scandal. He then closed the book. "Tuesday no one was taken . . . why?"

No one could answer.

Max had left, he feared what Mr. Giles would do to them. The newspaper articles were left in the huge library. All were impressed by its contents. They left to join the others. They saw Louie running towards them as they approached him.

"I got my trinket", he kept telling them, "opera glasses, good ones . . . and $100,000. Am I lucky or what?"

"I certainly hope so Louie," Warren said.

"What have you all been doing?'

"Patricia has been very helpful with her knowledge of the occult, reading through incantations in some of the ancient books belonging to Giles helping us to understand how he's earthbound."

"And I tagged along reading through articles and other material about us and that includes everyone here."

"It was a help Father", Warren said, "encouraging."

After an hour Warren returns to his room to shower and rest. After he showered, notes began to appear again on the toilet paper, then before he could reach for a towel more notes appeared on it and then on the mirror. He assumed these notes were from Giles. He found a robe covering himself when his clothes had been written on as well. He carefully unrolled the toilet paper that was written on and placed the notes on a table. The towel was carefully draped across a chair, he wrote down what was on the mirror. When he returned to the bathroom more notes on toilet paper appeared. Again he unrolled the section written on. Then forgetting he was only in a robe went downstairs to find Max. There were whistles and clapping. Max was amused.

"You should be resting Sheriff."

"Besides being unnerving, Giles is leaving me notes everywhere, on toilet paper, towel, mirror, my clothes . . . I can't keep up trying to save everything he's written. I'll transcribe everything to paper, but this has got to stop."

"Fortunately Mr. Giles still has a sense of humor, what can I do Sheriff?"

If you could ask him to meet with me and dictate any information he feels pertinent to this case, I'll write it down . . . easier and faster. I also need another towel, toilet paper and clothes."

"You'll have them directly. I'll advise Mr. Giles of your request." Max knew the Sheriff had to rest in spite of Mr. Giles' timetable. "I'll be up later to clean your wounds after you rest."

Warren had rested very little in an attempt to record on paper all the notes left by Giles and interview those he hadn't yet. Plans were now moving forward for an escape attempt. He rested for an hour then went downstairs. Max changed his bandages.

Father Benjamin was playing cards. Warren had an ally in him willing to help where he could.

"Father, I need to ask you a few questions when you have a moment."

He finished the hand, "Not winning today," he said.

"Appreciate your help. How did you know Giles Macfarland?"

"I was a priest at All Saints Catholic Church where Mr. Macfarland attended. He supported special programs then, programs that helped young boys to become men, that's about it. I saw him about four weeks ago at a gala here, read about his death three days later."

"Did you two have a disagreement, a falling out about anything?"

"No, everything was good."

Warren, however, had read the article about Father Benjamin. "Why does Giles consider you to be a suspect?"

"Honestly, I don't know."

Warren didn't believe the priest. "Thank you sir," Warren said and left.

Dinner was served and they all ate together in the parlor.

Tess told them about her trinket, "A $2,000 Versace dress and the money.

"Anyone else?" Warren asked.

Jason Jackson pretended he didn't receive a trinket or the money when in reality he did, a get out of jail free card from a Monopoly Game and the money as well.

"Patricia?" Marilyn asked.

"I got a very old book on the occult, not that book we're searching for but this one is a century old in mint condition, the money was inside it."

"I was given a doctor's bag filled with notes and the instruments used when I operated on Mr. Giles' late wife. I was so startled that the money seemed unimportant," Dr. Fashad told them.

They enjoyed being together and still believed that a rescue would come.

That evening Warren was preparing for bed, it was late. He heard his door open. Something stood behind him, it was an ominous feeling.

"Are you Giles?" he asked.

"I am".

Warren wouldn't turn around.

"How are you feeling?" Giles asked him.

"Strange, I don't know, confused."

"That will pass."

"I was fortunate, I didn't die." He was testing Giles by saying this.

"Only you did. Max found you, we brought you back . . . . why aren't we facing each other? Surely there have been crime scenes to equal how my deteriorating body looks, no surprise to you."

Warren reluctantly turned and faced Giles who now moved closer into the dim light given by a lamp. Warren just stood there staring at Giles for a moment then passed out. He came to minutes later.

"Too much, too soon," Giles said.

"No, I'm ok, just weak . . . you didn't take anyone Tuesday."

"Then should I take two on Thursday?"

"I'll do my best Giles but we need more time."

"All right".

The toilet paper notes and all notes from Giles would be transcribed to a note pad seen only by Warren. They worked together as Warren sat up in bed as he continued to recover and took dictation for over an hour. The sight of a deceased, decaying Giles Macfarland had unnerved him and realizing that he himself had been brought back from the dead was incomprehensible.

"Giles, will you kill all these people if your murderer isn't found?"

"Yes, one of them is my murderer."

"And me?"

Giles turned to him not answering the question. "Rest, you will need it." Then he left.

The next day Warren had someone's life to save not knowing who would die next. He had hoped that Giles would give him more time before someone else would be terminated. He asked Max at length about the guests and now realized that he had played a part in restoring his life. He would thank him at the proper time. The guests grew nervous believing that one would die that day. Dante and two others met with Warren. Max knew that something was up.

"Max, this meeting is private," Warren said. He was puzzled but left the room.

"When?"

"In an hour get everyone away from the doors," Dante said.

Mr. Giles talked with Max. "They are going to blow the front doors, fools, I know every move they make."

"What can I do to stop it?"

"Nothing, one will die."

The hour passed, Dante blew the huge oak front doors off their hinges, debris went in every direction. Angie Chang at that moment walked into the room suddenly and was hit and killed by a piece of debris. Daniel rushed to revive her but to no avail. The hole blown out of the house along with the doors was huge. They could now see outside but discovered that there was still an unseen force keeping them inside, keeping them from being seen and freedom. Gradually darkness covered what they were able to see outside like a black curtain.

Warren took this especially hard when he had encouraged the others to do this and the loss of Angie was tragic.

Giles became so angry with Warren that he waits for him in his room. Warren arrives devastated. Giles spoke to him. "Angie Chang might have lived, no one was going to die today, but you and the others with your aberrant behavior killed her blowing the doors off their hinges. I liked Angie. You were the instigator were you not?"

Warren faced Giles, "I was."

Giles then walked toward him. "Everything has a consequence. Everyone has buried in their thoughts some tragedy, their worst moment." He held Warren against a wall. "I am forcing you to remember the worst moment in your life, the thing you have buried deep in your mind."

Warren's mind flooded with memories of a police matter gone bad. He struggles to not remember.

"Tell me," Giles demanded.

"Giles stop." Warren struggled.

"Tell me."

"A police sting in a Texas border town . . ."

"Continue."

"We had planned this for months, my partner infiltrated a drug cartel from Mexico but she hadn't contacted us in several hours . . . those of us trying to get to her were pinned down by gunfire. My partner waited . . . for me, we couldn't get to her. No more Giles," Warren pleaded.

"What happened to her?"

Warren was now hyperventilating, his heart beat faster as he relived the moment. "I found her first, bound and mutilated, dying . . . she looked into my eyes . . . I loved her." Tears flowed, his seemingly hardened exterior had been fractured.

Giles now stopped. "I won't go further." He continued to hold Warren against the wall for several minutes then released him. "Now no more deception. Continue the investigation, convince them to be forthcoming, they trust you. No more escape attempts. I'll tell you more about the guests later if you're up to it." Giles left. Warren just stood against the wall for a few moments trying to compose himself. Max came upstairs to administer antibiotics and clean the wounds sustained by the earlier attempt on his life.

"What did he say to you Sheriff?" As he asked this he knew Warren had been disciplined.

"Don't ask."

The body of Angie Chang had been moved to the vault in the basement by all involved. Marilyn was there along with Father Benjamin who said a prayer. She couldn't get any response from Warren.

"Max?"

"He'll tell you when he's ready, don't press him for answers just yet."

Later Patricia decided to conduct her séance. Warren, still feeling the discipline Giles exacted on him, decided to sit in to protect her if it became necessary.

"Father Benjamin?"

"I'll sit this one out," he told her.

Warren, Dante, Marilyn, Bradley, Louie and Daniel all sat with Patricia.

"Hold hands."

Warren and Dante, sitting next to each other traded places, not wanting to hold hands they put Marilyn in the middle. Patricia had placed one of Mr. Giles' books on the occult in the center of the table. He had given her this book as a trinket gift. She placed a candle by it. She went into her séance like a pro, following almost like a script in a scary movie.

She named each person in the house with the exception of the staff. The words, "We beseech you," brought out noises like wind and twisting pipe. Marilyn's fingernails dug into Warren.

"Sorry," she whispered.

"We ask you to show yourself, show us mercy."

"Maybe he can't hear us," Louie said wearing a pink robe.

"Mr. Giles Macfarland, I summon you."

Nothing happened.

"Oh well," Dante remarked.

Patricia then rolled her eyes as if in a trance, a voice spoke though her, a different voice.

"My murderer is here among you. Until the guilty one is found, all of you will remain here with me."

Suddenly the table shook. Patricia came out of the trance. No one said a word for a few moments.

"What happened?" Patricia asked.

Dante replied, "Cheap theatrics."

"Wait and see," she said.

Warren stayed to talk with Patricia.

"I didn't kill Giles."

"I never said you did. How did you know him?"

"I sold houses as a real estate agent for a mortgage company. The construction of these homes was quick, unfortunately too quick. The wiring was faulty, Giles' brother died in a fire."

"Did you report what you discovered?"

"Why yes."

"Yet you stayed on."

"Only to gather evidence."

Warren knew she was lying, giving Giles a reason to discredit her or worse. He contemplated what course of action to take as he felt overwhelmed by the magnitude of the situation, two deaths, another tonight.

He returned to his room and prepared for dictation. Giles entered and sat in a chair by Warren who sat up in bed writing whatever Giles decided to dictate.

"Max told me your wounds were healing quickly. Three days alive now . . . two deaths, one tonight."

"Is Patricia next on your calendar of events?" Warren asked bluntly.

"I really don't know, perhaps I should choose one now."

"Don't take Louie."

"Why not?"

"I haven't seen him perform."

Giles realized that in his attempt to punish Warren he hadn't broken his will or sense of humor, this pleased him.

That evening after Giles left, Warren had a restless night. He wanted to find a way out of the situation, wanted to protect Marilyn most of all. Some slept in the parlor together for safety issues, a few in their respective rooms. Some played cards to pass the time afraid to sleep but drifted off as the hours ticked away to midnight.

Suddenly a noise moved through the great house like rushing water or wind. Patricia had been attempting to conjure up Giles. She held a candle and opened her door to the hall. Warren's room was up the hall near the stairs, she didn't disturb him as she walked toward a portrait of Mr. Giles where the hall ended. Drawn to it, she placed the book of incantations, given to her, below the portrait and with her candle sat on the floor; she began reading quietly as she summoned Mr. Giles. Within minutes the portrait seemed to come alive, Giles literally stepped out of the portrait and stood beside her. For a moment she couldn't move, couldn't scream. He touched her arm and pulled her to her feet.

"You summoned me?" he asked. "I'm here to show you the book you've been looking for."

No one heard anything, no one would come for her. Everyone had been put in a deep sleep including Max and the staff so as not to hear Patricia's screams as she tried to escape Giles. He took her into the library.

"I didn't murder you," she cried.

"You caused others to die including my brother. Faulty wiring, cover-ups, payoffs. What are you going to do Patricia when you can't spend the money because you're dead?"

"I admit it, I'm guilty. No one was supposed to die."

"My brother was crippled and couldn't reach the exit in time . . . that was tantamount to murder."

"Show me where your power comes from."

"The book you speak of is on that table. That's how I returned. Open it, read from it."

She forgot to be afraid as she began reading it. The words in Latin suddenly became English. As she read on she felt her body go limp, she fell. Giles then closed the book, picked her up, placed her in a chair, kissed her then left with the book. Passing the clock in the hall it was five minutes till midnight.

Morning came. Warren was awakened.

"Sheriff, downstairs in the library, Patricia has died," Max told him.

Everyone gathered around Daniel who quickly determined that she died of fright. "Her heart literally stopped."

"I didn't hear a thing," Bradley said, "no screams, nothing."

"Neither did I," Warren said as he looked around at everyone for signs of foul play.

They moved her body to the vault then Father Benjamin said a prayer. When they went upstairs they discussed what they might do, what options were left for an escape knowing that Warren was seeing Giles everyday to take dictation regarding the suspects, wondering if he knew who would die next. They had coffee as the discussion went on.

"Tell us you've discovered who murdered Giles Macfarland."

"I can't, I won't lie to you, not everyone has been interviewed and their involvement with Giles disclosed."

Warren then talked to Max privately. "No one will know what I'm about to ask you, but this book that Patricia mentioned, is it here?"

"I will tell you what I know and why I said earlier that no one would ever find that book. I walked by Mr. Giles' study one day taking a break from my schooling. He had this book, a very old book, sitting on his desk, it was written in Latin. I learned Latin in medical school. I opened a latch that should have locked it. Had Mr. Giles forgotten to lock it, I don't know. I began to read the first page, there was a sense of evil emanating from it. Suddenly I began to feel drained, tired, I kept reading for several minutes. Mr. Giles found me, he closed the book quickly, for a few moments he couldn't reach me, then I came to myself. He was relieved and then gave me a stern warning not to touch it again, not to read from it. There was genuine fear in him, he had never chided me before, ever. From then on I never saw it again or asked. He said it was evil. I believe he destroyed it as he intended. He has enormous power from some source but I don't know from what. You saw several books in his library on the occult but you will never find that one. I hope this has been some help to you Sheriff."

"It has Max."

Bradley had collaborated with Warren by helping him sort evidence and information comparing what they knew so far about each person. The information was stored in a computer for comparisons. Pictures from the camera phones documenting each person there living or now deceased were fed into the computer—no internet had been allowed so police files couldn't be tapped into for background checks on each guest.

Father Benjamin and Tess had spent hours in the library reading about Giles, learning more about his background even though they had known him over the years, perhaps to find any weakness or anything they might use to escape.

Giles met with Warren earlier that day for dictation.

"It's not a fair fight Giles."

"I didn't say it would be. Everyone must see themselves as they really are."

"Did Patricia see herself or you as you really are?"

Giles didn't answer except to say, "Let's begin."

A half hour into dictation Giles stops suddenly. "Get the men off the roof! They are attempting to raise an antenna and send a signal to the authorities. Were you in on this?"

"Hell no!" Warren said as he quickly got off the bed throwing his notes to the side leaving Giles as he attempted to save the men. Max heard the commotion and followed.

The antenna was in place. Jason was preparing to send the signal. Bradley and Daniel were standing by, a collaboration of their efforts.

"Get off the roof now!" Warren shouted to the three.

"We've done it Sheriff," Bradley said.

"Giles knows it, don't send that signal."

The sky was clouding up, the wind blew harder. Jason glances at Warren as he completes the last detail.

"Come inside before Giles kills one or all of you."

Jason confesses to Warren, "I did it, I killed them."

"I know, come inside, we'll talk".

"Ten years wasn't enough not by any stretch. I was on PCP, wasn't in my right mind . . . my parents, my little sister. You knew it was me all along. My lawyer convinced me to play the race card, the conviction was overturned after you convinced the D.A. to convict me on circumstantial evidence. Ten years wasn't enough," he repeated again.

"Let's talk about it."

"I'd like to first send this signal."

"Giles knows it."

Jason smiles then presses the button to begin the signal. Lightening at that moment strikes the antenna instantly killing Jason. His body was charred, burned beyond recognition. In a while Max brought blankets to wrap the body. Bradley, Daniel and Warren then moved him downstairs. Everyone was aware that Jason give his life to help free them but to no avail. Warren had a beer to calm himself. Max was passing out anything to calm their nerves. Daniel and Bradley felt defeated and out of options.

"Mr. Giles is nothing more than a supernatural killing machine," Daniel remarked. Bradley and Warren agreed.

"Jason was a brave man," Warren said. "You guys try to hang in there. I'll be back in an hour or so." He went upstairs to where Giles was waiting and said nothing as he sat on the bed once again to take dictation.

"Are you all right?" Giles asked him.

"Not really, what's all right about electrocuting a man to death? Ready when you are." Warren's dislike for Giles was very evident.

"Do you want to save the others?" Giles asked.

"What do you think I've been trying to do?" he asked frustrated and angry. "You want your revenge, I want to give it to you."

"I believe you," Giles replied. "Then do as I ask and continue our collaboration with the ongoing investigation."

"Ready," Warren said.

"Then let's begin. Louie Lamour Zimmerman, brilliant actor adopted the middle name Lamour after his favorite actress Dorothy Lamour. Was a struggling actor with an alcohol problem. I bank rolled a production in New York and hired him for the lead role. Being an alcoholic caused him to miss performances, forget his lines; after a month, I fired him. He got help, gradually put his alcohol abuse behind him, became a gay activist."

"Did you feel threatened by him?"

"No, and I gave him another chance in a new production, he did very well. He and Tess will perform tomorrow night if you're interested."

"Is Tess a performer?"

"Come and you'll find out."

"Giles, none of these people had any serious motivation for killing you, I'm a good judge of people."

"I'm sure you are."

Warren hesitated then, "Tell me about yourself."

"Why on earth?"

"It might be helpful to the case."

CHAPTER VI

Giles and Max

"I know you're from London. Graduated from Oxford. Doctorates in the medical field and science, became a surgeon, moved to America, ended up in Houston, became a philanthropist. Built your empire from humble beginnings. Married . . ."

"I'll take it from here", Giles said. "I married an American girl, a teacher in 1970. All our attempts at having children were disastrous, all stillborn. Mary was her name, she died in childbirth as well as the child. This moved me more into the field of scientific and medical research. I moved into this place of refuge appearing at various functions. I've broken ground on many projects, the hospitals became like children I had spawned. Art galleries and museums were things I became interested in. The curator at the Museum Van Het Broodhuis, in Brussels, became a friend of mine. He gave me a rare book on the Dark Arts. Being curious but being Catholic I hesitated . . . curiosity got the better of me. It became a ritual. This allowed me to survive here as a spirit. There were women in my life, I never found Mary in any of them. I later met Max Fogel, a student at Rice University. He had emigrated from Germany at 17, his parents were deceased. Beginning his studies for doctorates in the medical and scientific fields we met when I was lecturing students as a guest speaker on the value of majoring in these two fields, the doors it could open and the scholarships I would be donating to the school for both. Max talked to me about someone to sponsor him. His scholarship was for science only and very limited, so I decided to sponsor him, he would live at the school take his classes and at the mansion on weekends where I would continue to teach him science and the medical field and he would work for me as my assistant in research. It was a grueling schedule; he contracted TB and almost died, my research became his salvation. He returned the favor years later as I became debilitated from a progressive disease which rendered my legs useless. Max and I exhausted every avenue to slow it or cure it. He hired a physical therapist and nurse to assist. Then as things got worse, Rupert, a long time friend of Max's agreed to help as I could no longer do research on a cure. The disease progressed quickly and at this rate I had a year. Parkinson's is a very painful disease. Max and Rupert worked tirelessly, even as exhaustion set in. Finally after weeks a possible cure."

"This will be painful," they told me, "with an anesthetic we can't judge how effective each shot will be."

"Then do it without," I told them.

"The shots were injected into the leg muscles, very painful. It wasn't a total cure but was very effective. Within a week I had begun physical therapy and was walking in two months. I met Marilyn Grant soon after at an art exhibit and decided to marry her. Max saw to all the details helping me prepare for my wedding. We discussed the fact that she might be marrying me for my money, we both had a good laugh knowing she was. Then a year later after a stem cell gala at the mansion, I was murdered. The night you were shot Max found you as I've already told you and alerted me. I came quickly and injected a paralyzing agent into your neck to sustain you but the agent would only last an hour. With his help you were brought back, he stayed hours assisting me. Calculations, discussions on how to proceed step-by-step, he was there. He deserves a lot more credit than he receives, people assume he is my valet and assistant, running this house and what transpires in it with efficiency, his choice, when in reality we have co-authored several books on research and articles on medical and scientific topics. He loves being around people fearing that his status as a doctor and scientist would inhibit the interaction he has with them."

Warren was in disbelief over hearing how he was brought back and Max's role in his resurrection.

"Max is like a son to me and a good listener."

"So he inherits from the research only?"

"Making him a millionaire several times over . . . content to stay with an aging scientist even if I am dead."

"For thirty-seven he appears younger."

"When I injected him with stem cells years ago it caused an angiogenesis effect, formation of new blood vessels, the blood flow rich in oxygen coursing throughout his entire body. He ages but now more slowly. People assume he's in his mid twenties."

"Why did you request me to investigate your murder?" Warren asked.

"I know a great deal about you Sheriff. Your father and brother were both in the Sheriff's Department. Your father brought you in when he was a sheriff. Your brother, a deputy, unfortunately was gunned down in a Mexico-Texas border town. Then you joined the department. You have had several close calls. A graduate with two masters degrees in Judicial and Criminal Law, the second in forensics, I heard you and Dante discussing this. You became sheriff in Austin then later sheriff at the High Crimes Bureau in Houston. Crime dropped dramatically. Not married yet, the right one will come along. I requested your help here because you are thorough. I know much more about you than you would reveal willingly to me. You try to see the cup half full, the best in a person. You would pursue the guilty into Hell if you had to. I needed your expertise here, your gut feeling about the guests. I'm not sure you'll find my killer but you're the best chance. Max isn't a suspect, he will help you in the investigation if needed. I deceived him, you and the others here as he sent personal invitations to the reading of the will even meeting with you personally to attend, he had no idea of my plan."

Warren knew Giles still had a conscience about his actions especially where it concerned his son. Warren was tired but willing to continue. "Tell me about Tess Donner."

"We'll continue this later, rest now."

Giles left.

Rest was inevitable. Two hours passed. After uninterrupted sleep Warren went downstairs to join the others. It was getting wild as Daniel and Bradley broke into song. Louie was playing the piano. Marilyn walked over to Warren.

"Everyone is enjoying themselves, beer?"

"Yes and whatever they're eating."

"How are you Sheriff?" Max asked.

"Better, took dictation earlier from Giles."

"And what did he tell you?"

"Seems I owe you my life."

"I was glad to help Sheriff, I . . ."

"I won't tell anyone, I should but I won't. Who looks guilty in here Max? Who killed Giles?"

"Dante Stephens would be number one on my list, proving it is another matter."

"My feelings exactly. Tell me if you hear anything."

"Will do."

Warren walked over to Tess. "Ms. Donner."

"Hello Sheriff, am I being interviewed now?"

"I'd appreciate it if you have the time."

"Nothing but time."

"Looking forward to you and Louie tomorrow evening."

"Good. May I begin by saying Giles meant a lot to me. I never would have harmed him. I met him years ago when I sang at the Metropolitan as a guest soloist. Giles helped me start my first fashion store which became ten stores in a five year period. I sang at his funeral. I loved him. I don't know why he had me brought here but he had his reasons."

"None of us really know why, to catch a murderer is one thing but this."

"Did I answer your questions?"

"Yes, it was a pleasure."

"Likewise."

"Sheriff, Mr. Giles would like to see you upstairs," Max told him, "when it's convenient."

"Headed that way."

Warren was back in his room and Giles was there waiting.

"Tess didn't tell you everything. Tess Donner Fashions, ten stores, a multi-millionaire at fifty. She and I were close. Tess then loses a fortune due to bringing in a partner who didn't know how to run a business, I had advised against her decision. I did bankroll part of her business. She came to me for more help but she wouldn't rid herself of the partner and I wouldn't help her again. She never forgot this. Her voice is extraordinary, sang at the Metropolitan as she told you. It was an event having her sing at my funeral."

"What about Dante Stephens and Marilyn?"

"Marilyn is about being wild and innocent, two sides of a coin, but you would know that, you left her, she married an old man who would give her anything she asked for. I wasn't able to satisfy her as a husband.

She and Dante hooked up a year ago, he was able to fulfill the needs that I couldn't and she would remain my wife. She did love me."

"And Dante?"

"Dante, as you discovered is an arrogant bastard, playboy, wealthy, inherited his father's demolition company, his father died under mysterious circumstances. A year younger than Marilyn, he has had a bad influence on her. Could he have murdered me, could he have fired three rounds into your abdomen, perhaps, where is the confession, the proof? Marilyn is no murderer."

"I agree, I've known her since childhood."

Giles knew they had made love the day everyone arrived at the mansion. If Dante was aware of Marilyn's liaison with Warren, he never revealed it.

"Good night Sheriff." Giles left.

Marilyn came to check on him. He was asleep. She still loved him.

Sunday was a new start. Would anyone die that day? Giles was the only one who knew. Not seeing a way out of the situation the remaining guests were nervous and had given up any escape attempts. Warren asked Giles about a deceased guest, Palmer Sparrow.

"Since I didn't get to interview him, I need to know why he might have had reason or reasons to murder you."

Giles replied, "All this man was good for was his O—blood transfused to you. Years ago he had been a rival of sorts for the affection of my wife Mary. He had owned one of the premier banks in Houston. I helped make that bank after I struggled for success and finally achieved it. I poured a million into its assets. Palmer Sparrow began some reckless investments with the money while foreclosing on those who couldn't pay off the bad loans he made to them. We argued, I withdrew everything, the bank never recovered, he was voted out as CEO. Later when he joined the Internal Revenue he had old records of my activities and doctored them to reflect badly on me. For several years he has pursued a case against me. The man's mental state was off. I grew tired of him, he had caused havoc and pain to others who couldn't afford lawyers to help and lost everything. I don't believe, however, he murdered me."

"Ok, scratch that one from the Most Wanted List," Warren quipped.

"You have a knack for sarcasm," Giles said then left.

Warren went downstairs joining the others. Breakfast was being served. He was observing everyone. Max was making the guests feel comfortable, Louie was playing the piano.

"Are you coming to watch the performance?" Louie asked Warren.

"Wouldn't miss it Louie."

"You know I'm right, people searching for us are seeing an illusion, they don't think we're here."

"I know."

"What do you miss most being trapped her?"

"Freedom, watching a sunrise, seeing my friends at the Bureau. I thought when we blew off the doors and realized we were still prisoners that we would at least see the outside, not this darkness surrounding this place."

"I have similar feelings. If we make it out I'll buy you a beer and tickets to my next performance."

"You're on Louie."

Each one of the guests talked with Warren about the murder of Giles and professed his or her innocence.

Dante entered the smaller kitchen very drunk. Mrs. Bradley had left with Max for a few minutes. Silvia was working to serve the guests. Dante watched her for a moment, thought how beautiful she was and came behind her with the intent of violating her in some way. As he was about to touch her, an arm reached in front of him suddenly.

"May I help you sir?"

Silvia turned suddenly seeing Max between her and Dante.

"No, everything is fine," Dante said disappointed and left.

"I never heard him enter the kitchen."

"That guy is bad news, I'll watch him more carefully."

The day went on, finally stretched into evening.

Tess and Louie did perform that night. It was Sunday. Even Dante appreciated the diversion. Everyone was wined and dined. She and Louie did their rendition of three scenes from 'La Cage Au Faux'. Both sang. Giles had been correct, both could act and sing. Everyone was feeling lucky to be alive, no one died that day. Father Benjamin had left during the third scene and hadn't returned, Warren noticed. Father Benjamin had found a ring earlier in his room and $100,000. He left for a part of the huge house he was drawn to, compelled to go to the library. He remembered that the ring belonged to a boy at his parish in the special 'Boys to Men' program helping young men to realize their dreams. He was a pedophile and pursued a boy causing him to die when he ran in front of a speeding car, he was hit, his ring was knocked off his finger. Father Benjamin tried to find the ring, the police were called. Rumors had circulated for years about the Father. Giles, who attended that parish, forced him to retire or face charges—he retired. Giles was now there with Father Benjamin in the library. Giles had opened a book with the boy's picture inside for him to see. Holding the ring Father Benjamin walked up the stairs to the second floor just as Warren and Max arrived.

"I caused him to die," he said.

Warren thought this was a confession to Giles' murder. Then Father Benjamin saw an image of the boy downstairs. He stood there repeating one phrase, "I'm sorry." Then he fell to his death.

Giles spoke but wasn't seen. "He caused a boy to die and killed what others might have become . . . he wasn't my murderer."

The others arrived as Warren and Max began moving the body. Blankets were brought.

"We didn't make the twenty-four hour mark," Daniel said.

No one else said a word.

Warren had wanted to discuss Angie Chang further with Giles telling him what she said but since inadvertently causing her death he didn't pursue it now.

CHAPTER VII

Confessions of a Murderer—Escape

That evening Warren began to come on to Marilyn where Dante could hear. "Remember what it felt like being with a real man?" He touches Marilyn sensually and they both go around a corner.

Dante sees this while he's playing cards, anxious and angry he then can't concentrate.

"Let's go upstairs," Warren said and kissed her.

"Dante is across the room, I don't think it's a good idea," Marilyn said.

Warren whispered, "Pretend like we did when we were role playing."

"To . . ."

"You'll see."

Dante seethed with anger, he then demanded a glass of wine. Max obliged, he had heard everything and talked to Mr. Giles.

"The Sheriff has put himself in danger coming on to Miss Marilyn and to make sure Dante has seen and heard everything, very deliberate."

Giles thought for a moment. "Clever chess move, Marilyn is the witness as the Sheriff tries to enrage Dante to force a confession. If it goes too far Dante might attempt to kill the Sheriff."

Dante went upstairs and entered Warren's room holding a pistol expecting to find both Warren and Marilyn engaged in making love. Instead Marilyn was sitting on the bed and Warren was sitting in a chair.

"Well what is going on?" he asked angrily pointing the weapon at Warren, Marilyn was listening to every word.

"I see you found my pistol, going to kill me again?"

"Most definitely."

Dante then walked over to Marilyn and slapped her, Warren stood up, knocked the pistol out of Dante's hand and backhanded him so hard that he fell to the floor, a fight ensued.

"I can take you," Dante said, "I'm a black belt."

"Ain't that a coincidence, so am I."

They fought.

"How did you do the old man? It took him three days to die."

Dante didn't answer.

"We know you did it, but how did you do it? Don't be modest Dante."

The fight escalated, broken mirrors, furniture.

Then, "One shot, sodium cyanide to his scalp, one injection."

"Three days in a coma," Warren said.

"He felt nothing."

"Are you sure?"

Just then the door to the room burst open, Giles walked in and in an instant pushed both Dante and Warren in different directions across the room. Warren for a moment saw Giles standing over Dante as he cut his throat and let him bleed to death. Then as Marilyn watched, Giles stood over a dazed Warren, he touched his face.

"Forget," he said. Then he turned to Max, "It's time." Giles shed his body and entered Dante. Max helped him complete the transition then bandaged his neck. Marilyn couldn't process this. Giles turned to her. "If you want to live come with me. Max move our Sheriff to the porch outside, get everyone moving in that direction then we leave the back way, we mustn't be seen."

A call was made, "There are survivors at the Macfarland Mansion, the Sheriff is there needing medical attention," referring to the bullet wounds Warren sustained earlier. "Search the basement, there are others who died." Max didn't give his name, he saw that Silvia had made it out. Reluctantly he left her behind as he, Giles and Marilyn escaped the police and their questions.

The mansion that earlier had appeared to not be there, only a field and broken gates, suddenly was visible again as the Sheriff's men and police arrived along with coroner and MICU personnel. Warren was dazed but he and the others made it out with tall tales of capture by a ghost. The staff of three women and surviving guests were found. Giles, in the body of Dante Stephens, Marilyn Macfarland and Max Fogel were missing along with the Cadillac belonging to Max. Warren was able to direct the police to the basement where the bodies were.

Everyone was questioned and gave the same answer. The ghost of Giles Macfarland held everyone captive until his murderer was found. He terminated several before the Sheriff learned the identity of the murderer and also must have been an illusionist to make the entire mansion disappear and then reappear it was reported. The Sheriff had been shot three times and someone other than Dr. Fashad with surgical skills was given credit for saving his life. Giles Macfarland's murderer Dante Stephens remained at large.

In a suburb of Houston in a large 20,000 square foot house were Giles, Marilyn and Max watching the Sheriff's press conference.

Months would pass, the Sheriff's report remained "Inconclusive." It was determined that Dante Stephens had shot Warren with his own pistol, a forty caliber Glock 22. Warren continued to carry it as a reminder of his death experience and obligation to protect and serve as possible.

CHAPTER VIII

New Lives—Finding Silvia

Things had become tense between Giles and Max, months had passed. Giles wasn't adjusting well to the young body now his. Max couldn't accept Giles this way, although he tried. He always thought of him as his father but now everytime he looked at Giles he saw a murderer, young and brash. Everyday he watched him losing control and the will to live. Max couldn't reconcile the deaths Giles had caused to the man who had mentored him and helped mold him.

"You don't believe I'm still Giles Macfarland in this body."

"Not the Mr. Giles I knew . . . I miss him."

"I did things I'm not proud of, I was always proud of you . . . six books on medical research we collaborated on, articles on scientific discoveries. As a young man you had a willingness to learn and a drive I haven't seen very often in young people. Your schooling and everything I taught you has made you more than my equal."

Max listened, his heart ached for the bond and friendship he had with Mr. Giles, but after taking the body of Dante Stephens he was different, distant, confused and had put important research on hold in favor of less important projects which could cost them the grant money if they didn't furnish the results in time.

"Max, what can I do?" Mr. Giles was frustrated as he asked this.

Max stopped taking readings off the computer which was giving crucial information, he didn't answer him, then he paced for a moment.

"I'll be back . . . late," he said.

Giles was concerned.

Later Giles and Marilyn ate dinner, he was very depressed, talked about making a new life with Marilyn and concerns about Max and their torn relationship. Mrs. Bradley who had figured things out about the new Mr. Giles was taking care of things at the 20,000 square foot mansion with a staff of three to assist her, she knew about everything that had transpired.

Max had called the Sheriff and asked to meet him at a local coffee shop. He was wearing his traditional all black shirt, trousers and suspenders.

"Good to see you Sheriff."

"And you Max or should I say Dr. Fogel?"

"Max is fine."

"How are things?" the Sheriff asked.

"I'm not adjusting to this. Mr. Giles is different, very different."

"He said you're the son he always wanted. If I could I'd have thrown him in jail, his methods were flawed. As a spirit he was angry. Taking the body of a murderer was an act of desperation. He has paid dearly Max, I'm sure he looks in the mirror every morning and sees the face of his murderer. You don't believe he's in there, he is, struggling to exist again as Giles. If you give him time he could be more the Giles you knew, not outwardly however."

"Every time I see him, I can't relax, can't feel the friendship, relationship we had, he won't continue our research."

"Whenever I saw Dante's face I wanted to slug him," Warren said. "Giles can't do it alone, help him Max."

Max struggled to not become emotional.

"Thanks for the coffee and the address."

"Hope you find her, watch your back, that area is dangerous, crime ridden, known for drug activity."

Max left, put his hair in a ponytail and drove his Cadillac convertible miles south to a community outside Houston. His mood lightened, now not as despondent he continued looking for someone he left months ago.

In the meantime at the mansion Giles was shaving, it was late that evening. The staff had gone to bed, Marilyn was asleep. As he looked in the mirror he pondered his decisions as he held the straight edge razor across his carotid artery, one cut and it would end. He cut into his neck slightly wounding himself then stopped, leaving the razor on the counter he went downstairs and drank a glass of wine hoping Max would return.

In over an hour Max arrived at a small community outside Houston after driving a hundred miles not having an exact address, it was dark. He was directed to a small house, knocked on the door. He heard music and talking in the background. A woman opened the door, seeing this tall man she called her husband.

"Forgive the late hour but is Silvia Diaz here?"

The woman talked with her husband in Spanish.

Then Max spoke telling them he was a friend. She called to her daughter Silvia. Silvia walked in, she was startled and almost fainted when she saw him. They embraced and kissed.

"I thought you were dead," she said.

"It's a long story."

"And I want to hear it."

She conversed with her mother and father in Spanish. Max joined in.

"You know Spanish?" Silvia asked.

"I learned it a few months ago, I'm fluent." Max had learned the language years ago but kept it from Silvia.

"Please sit down," her father said.

Her two younger brothers were outside looking in and also protecting the car belonging to Max. Curious onlookers were being kept away by the boys who carried baseball bats.

"Silvia, I want to ask you something." He held her hand. "You aren't taken? No ring?"

"I held out hope that you would come back to me . . . I thought you were dead, months went by, tell me where you have been?"

"I haven't been totally honest with you." Max began to tell her a story about fleeing the police after being freed from the mansion, now only speaking in English to not worry her parents.

"I could have gone with you," she said.

"No, I had to take Mr. Giles, I mean Dante and Miss Marilyn away from there to protect them from the police and their questions, several were murdered there. I knew you would be safe as would the Sheriff and the others who made it out."

"Be totally honest with me Max, what are you into? You told me something about research and the medical field, I thought you were kidding."

"I am a doctor and a scientist. Mr. Giles mentored me, we did research together and I was in charge of the household at the Macfarland mansion coordinating the staff and all activities which was another thing I enjoyed doing for Mr. Giles."

"I find all of this hard to believe."

"I thought it would get in the way, I didn't want you to care about titles, just care about me."

"I do."

"And I'm thirty-seven, too old?"

She smiled then, "Not too old, you look and act younger."

Max opened a box containing a ring. "I want to marry you."

Outside, some of the neighborhood kids tried to take parts from the car but again Silvia's brothers wouldn't allow it.

"He is going to be our brother-in-law," they replied, "hands off the car," as they continued watching through the window.

Silvia's parents gasped when they saw the ring. Mr. Diaz stood up and walked over to Max who asked him for his permission to marry her. He and Mrs. Diaz agreed.

"What do you say Silvia?" Max asked her.

She was in shock, "It's beautiful."

After looking into her eyes for a few moments he closed the box and handed it to her knowing that his leaving her had damaged the relationship, there were trust issues involved.

"Do you love me?" he asked.

"Yes, very much . . . this is a lot to process."

"I would make you a good husband and provider. I have been faithful Silvia, no other."

"I work and take care of Raoul and Ramirez. My mother and father have health issues, he works. I need to be able to check on them daily, so if I move . . ."

"We can deal with that."

"My education isn't complete. I had begun pre-nursing courses at a community college some time ago."

Silvia's parents were now motioning to her to say 'yes'.

"There is much I can teach you about the medical field as you are taking your courses."

"Where would we live?"

"I'm going to wait on that one, I must leave. Here's my cell phone number." She gave Max hers. "Keep the ring whether you say 'yes' or 'no'. If it's convenient I would like to stop by tomorrow evening maybe I'll have your answer then. He kissed her then left. The boys talked with Max.

"Which one of you is Ramirez?"

"He is, I am Raoul. Are you going to marry her?"

"I hope so, then you both would be my brothers-in-law. I'll be back tomorrow evening." He left.

"Who was that?" A man asked the boys, he had been watching Max.

"He wants to marry Silvia, he's coming back tomorrow," Ramirez told him.

"Then I'll have to speak with him when he returns."

Max felt an urgency about Mr. Giles and drove quickly. A hundred miles seemed like an eternity as he thought of him. He entered the mansion an hour later and found Mr. Giles sitting in a chair asleep in the parlor. Seeing the wound on his neck Max knew he had contemplated suicide. Giles woke up as Max was cleaning and bandaging the wound.

"Glad you're back."

"Good to be back, you got too close," referring to the cut with the razor. They proceeded to talk into the night, it was an emotional time especially when Giles heard about a possible wedding.

"I'll be here to support you whatever the outcome," Max told him.

"This transition has been hard for me but hardest on you Max and Marilyn. Our research has suffered but we must get back to it."

"You'll adjust, we'll all adjust and get you through this, don't do anything irrational," he pleaded. Max was sitting in a chair facing Mr. Giles. "I think of you as my father, always have. When you were murdered my world fell apart, then suddenly you were still here."

"I didn't want to leave you Max. My decision to hold those people was bordering on insanity and my anger caused me to inflict pain and suffering on them and everyone else . . . this was due in part to studying that hellish book on the occult, that won't be a problem again."

Max became very emotional, the tears flowed, he couldn't conceal it. Giles leaned over to him and as he held his face, kissed him on the forehead.

"Things will get better and if you and Silvia decide to stay here, you'll have a place with Marilyn and me indefinitely. We'll continue our research. I won't be leaving you again, not for a very long time." Giles began to tear up. Marilyn was out of sight listening, she too became emotional as she realized that Giles wasn't Dante, he loved her, he loved Max and the family would continue to heal.

Giles would gradually take control of the body he was in. To no longer be known by the word 'bastard' given to Dante. He would mold the body to fit his needs. His eight-five year old mind now realized he could love Marilyn totally.

The next evening Max returned to Silvia. As he left his car, suddenly he was surrounded by several men and escorted into a large barn that the small community shared. Raoul and Ramirez weren't sure what was about to happen. Once inside he was surrounded again while another man around six feet tall, muscular, in his thirties approached, he seemed very angry.

"What is this?" Max asked him.

"This is a test to see if you have the metal to fight me, if you win you marry Silvia. I am Hector Flores, her cousin."

"And if I lose?"

"Then you need to get out of her life and stay out."

"Does she have a say in this contest?"

"No, she knows nothing about it."

He then started walking around Max who saw no way out of this. Hector then threw the first punch knocking Max against a post. He didn't expect Max to defend himself.

"This is going to be easy," Hector said as he turned to the men surrounding them. He then leveled two more knocking Max to the floor. Raoul and Ramirez, who had stayed hidden, had climbed into the loft of the barn and were distressed over this contest.

Max wiped the blood from his face, "I deserved that for leaving her." Then he threw the next punch knocking Hector against the wall, the impact winded him and surprised him.

"Not bad but not good enough."

"What is good enough? How far is this going to go?"

"Until I say it's over, you fight or take your white ass back to Houston."

Hector delivered a blow with his foot knocking Max to the floor face down. Max countered quickly turning on his side and raised up on one arm kicked Hector hard in the chest knocking him back and to the floor. He hadn't expected Max to have any fighting ability and to walk away from the fight.

"Walk away while you can," Hector said.

"You could work out your frustrations as I did, daily kickboxing," Max said delivering another punch.

"I learned street fighting and karate in the army defending myself and my family," Hector said as he delivered a kick to his leg.

"And you're still defending them against anyone who tries to get close."

"Why shouldn't I? Silvia deserves better. She's been upset for months."

The fighting was intense and went on for twenty minutes, both were exhausted, breathing hard, bloodied and still standing studying each other as they drank water.

"That last one should have broken your ribs," Hector said.

"I love Silvia . . . it wasn't my intent to hurt her."

"I know, however this ends tonight and all the lies you've been telling her, that you're a doctor and a research scientist."

Max wouldn't quit, the fight continued. The circle of men surrounding both Hector and Max were now cheering for both as their cell phone cameras had recorded the action from the beginning. Suddenly there was a scream. Raoul had fallen from the loft, the fight stopped. Max went over to the boy, initially pushed away he convinced them that he could help. No one believed he was a doctor. One of the men got Silvia.

"Someone take my keys, bring the black case in the trunk." The boy wasn't breathing. "I need clean towels, alcohol, a knife." Several switch blades were offered by the men there. Max picked one sterilizing it quickly with tequila. "I need some small plastic tubing and duct tape, quickly." Several became involved. Silvia came with supplies, she was crying. "Someone call 911."

Everyone gave Max a strange look.

"There is no 911 out here," Hector said. "The nearest hospital is fifty miles away."

Max worked feverishly to save Raoul.

Silvia cried, "Don't let him die." She saw both Hector and Max bloodied and bruised and knew there had been a fight, it made her angry.

"Hector, I need your help here." Max was attempting to perform a tracheostomy enabling Raoul to breathe through a tube but his injured, bloodied hands were almost useless, he couldn't steady his hands for this delicate procedure. Hector was holding the boy steady. "I can't steady my hands, more light." Max was frustrated. Three work lamps were helping him to see more clearly.

Hector then steadies Max's hand as he says, "You're his only chance."

Max tries again, the incision was made, the tube inserted, Raoul began to breathe. Max listened to the boy's chest.

"Three broken ribs, probably a punctured lung . . . I can't be sure, we need a splint for his broken arm." One was quickly made.

"Is he going to make it?" Hector asked.

"I don't know, let's go, my car."

Hector sat by Max with Raoul in his arms holding the breathing tube steady. Silvia sat by him trying to remain calm. Her parents sat in the back seat with Ramirez. Max pressed the car to go as fast as possible. The GPS gave him an exact location of the hospital. He then called the Chief of Surgery, a friend of Mr. Giles to meet him there.

"I'm Dr. Fogel assistant to the late Dr. Giles Macfarland. A member of my fiancé's family has been severely injured in a fall. I need a trauma team waiting for us when we arrive, the boy could die." Max discussed his diagnosis and treatment given once they arrived.

"Looks like you need doctoring as well," the chief surgeon told Max looking at his bruised face and bloodied nose.

"A hazard of the trade, a patient with anger issues."

He didn't know if this was an attempt to lighten the mood.

"I'll see you in the O.R. Dr. Fogel."

Max got everyone settled and made his way to the O.R. to assist in the surgery.

Silvia talked with Hector. "What were you doing to Max?"

"Convincing him to leave and not come back. He kicks like a mule when he fights." This was a lopsided compliment.

"I want this to stop, see what it caused? I can think for myself. I don't care if you trust him or not, I'm going to marry him." She touched his face softly. "You're a good man Hector, hot headed at times."

It was now 3:00 a.m., hours had passed.

Max was back and talked to Mr. and Mrs. Diaz, Silvia and Hector were listening.

"Twenty-four hours will tell. He did have severe injuries."

Then he sat by Silvia with bags of ice for himself and Hector to help the swelling in their bruised faces.

Nothing was said for a few moments then, "I do," she said.

"What Silvia?" Max was exhausted.

"I want to marry you if this hasn't turned you away."

"Are you kidding? I haven't fought physically for anyone I loved, ever. I've been faithful only to you. I want to win back your trust." She kissed him, they held hands and slept.

He dreamed of when he first met Silvia a few months ago. As head and coordinator of the staff and events planner at the mansion he had a way of helping Mr. Giles as well as in the research they collaborated on. When he was hiring more staff, a young lady, Silvia Diaz, came for her interview for household staff personnel. There she was, he was sitting at a desk. He had chosen her before the interview began.

"Pretty Girl," was all he could think as he stood up. "Hello Ms. Diaz, I am Max Fogel."

"Nice to meet you, here is my resume."

"It says you are twenty-six, single, you live outside Houston?"

Max didn't know exactly where she lived, only a P. O. Box number.

"Yes, in a suburb called Camp."

"Any references?"

"Yes."

"You will be living here for much of the time."

"I understand."

"Then glad to have you as part of our staff."

As time went by, several months later, Max talks with Silvia. "I would like to get to know you better, there is no pressure—if you feel the same then after your shift meet me at my room."

Silva came not knowing what to expect. She told him, "Gloria Estefan is a favorite."

He played Gloria Estefan, they both liked similar things. As he talked with her they danced slowly then . . . "Are you sure?" he asked her.

She removed her shirt. He picked her up quite easily, at 5 foot 7 and he was 6 foot 2 and placed her on the bed, they made love. Over time they developed a deep friendship and love for one another.

At one point he told her she was "the most anatomically correct woman he had ever seen."

"Based on what?" she asked startled at the statement.

"Working with cadavers," he said.

"Max, you have a strange sense of humor," not knowing at that time he was doctor.

He helped out as he could with the staff.

"He doesn't know Spanish," Silvia told Mrs. Bradley who had been hired by Max six years earlier. Max was on a small ladder placing dishes on the top shelf, he was listening.

"He does," Mrs. Bradley said.

"I'll prove it," Silvia said. She began to tell something about Max.

"Oh no Silvia", he thought, his brown eyes grew larger as he was listening, he dropped a dish.

Silvia then told Mrs. Bradley, "See he doesn't speak Spanish."

"Excuse me ladies," he said, "I'll attend to this." He cleaned up the broken dish.

"What were you about to say? Finish please," Mrs. Bradley said.

"No, not necessary, I've proved my point," Silvia said.

She never believed Max when he told her one day about being a doctor and a scientist doing research with Mr. Giles but she pretended that she did and certainly didn't believe he was thirty-seven.

Max woke up as the sun's rays began to shine through the hospital window, he checked on Raoul. The hospital extended the welcome mat for the family to stay as long as Raoul remained in I.C.U. Mr. Giles had started this hospital ten years earlier and continued to support it through the efforts of his research with Max.

Max had called Mr. Giles earlier about the events of the evening. He and Silvia discussed plans as they stayed at the hospital.

"Would it be agreeable for your family to move to Houston, that includes Hector if he is willing."

This surprised Silvia.

"You and I will be living at the mansion if you agree to this, where 20,000 square feet will give all of us the room we need, even if temporary. Mr. Fairlane, my uncle and I will continue research, you continue your education, get your degree."

Silvia thought about this carefully.

"That ring on your finger symbolizes a partnership between us."

"I'll discuss this with my parents. Raoul and Ramirez, they will be willing . . . Hector I don't know."

They kissed.

The next week Silvia left with Max. Her parents picked out a house that he paid for, no strings attached. Raoul continued to heal.

Later the pictures of the fight between Hector and Max appeared on U-Tube. Max became very well known. "The Doctor Who Kickboxes" was the title. Silvia was impressed as she, Raoul and Ramirez watched the fight and knowing he fought for her.

Mr. Giles had a talk with Max about the incident but he was proud of his son, he had also seen the video.

Max got a call from Sheriff Warren, "You're famous, want to teach me some of those moves? I warned you not to go out there." He laughed.

When Silvia saw Mr. Giles again, Max introduced him as Mr. Giles' step-brother Giles Fairlane. She was shocked that he looked like Dante Stephens, she was confused but courteous to him. They talked privately.

"His hair and . . ."

"There are things I will tell you that you will know in time. Just accept that he is my uncle and a good person, one of those trust things."

"I will," she said as she looked into his brown eyes.

CHAPTER IX

Max and Silvia Marry

Max and Silvia prepared for their wedding at the mansion. Mr. Giles was his best man and Rupert his groomsman. Veronica and Marilyn sat on either side of Warren. There were over a hundred in attendance. There was a classical guitarist and flutist for the instrumental. Silvia then walked down the aisle wearing a floor length white silk and lace gown, Vera Wang design and veil made of lace forming a small train as it draped over her gown, her father gave her away to Max. She had two cousins as maid of honor and bridesmaid. Raoul and Ramirez were ring bearers. 'Here Comes the Bride' was played briefly then a Gloria Estefan song. When she and Max stood before the priest and looked into each other's eyes, it was as if their souls became one.

Earlier he had talked to Mr. Giles. "Are you ready Max?"

"How can I make her happy?"

"Are you committed to her?"

"Yes, I love her deeply, it was never like this until Silvia."

"Be yourself Max, everything will fall into place."

Afterward there was a reception to wine and dine everyone. The music was an eclectic mix. Warren and Veronica were getting it on. Mr. Giles danced with Marilyn, he felt very close to her that evening.

CHAPTER X

Trip to Germany—'The Book'

The curator of the Museum Van Het Broodhuis in Brussels, Belgium, a friend of Mr. Giles was dying and wanted the book on the Dark Arts given back. He pleaded with Giles then demanded that he return the book.

"It has been years since you gave it to me, I no longer have it Klauss, I gave it to a museum here in Houston . . . it was later reported missing. I heard you weren't well, haven't seen you in several years."

"Giles, I know you, you stayed earthbound when you died months ago, that book you read from allowed you to do it. You have the book. I need it."

"Since you know of my experience I won't bother denying it, but I don't have the book."

"Then I will be forced to pressure you to return it." Klauss had grown belligerent toward Giles. "I will take something precious from you and destroy it for your deceit."

Giles couldn't believe his friend had turned on him and had threatened him. His mind turned to Max and Silvia who were touring Max's native Germany. Klauss ended the call. Was Marilyn in danger?

Max and Silvia, a very pregnant Silvia, were now in Berlin. He showed her where he grew up living with an uncle after his parents were killed. "I emigrated at seventeen with my Uncle's permission to America, attended Rice University, met Mr. Giles who essentially adopted me, I was very fortunate, he taught me courses in science, research and in the medical field."

"Were you scared? You were so young in a new country."

"Yes I was, but Mr. Giles promised to mentor me as he put me through school. Now I'm a doctor and a scientist like him, I can help people; by the way, you're doing well on your courses."

"I love going to school again and I love the thought of being a mother."

"You still like your OBGYN?"

"Very much."

"You know I could . . ."

"No Max, not this, no substitute."

"Well all right then."

"Let's go for lunch."

"I have the strangest feeling that we're being followed," Max said, he was intuitive as always.

"I don't see anyone, when did you sense this?"

"Ever since we arrived at the airport three days ago."

"The food here is very good, I've never had German food before."

"This restaurant is very old and the German food is totally authentic."

They laughed, Silvia felt the baby moving. Max touched her stomach, he smiled. "Is it a little Max or Silvia?"

"Six months and counting," she said, "and I don't know the sex."

They left an hour later and were walking in an area crowded with people and cars. Suddenly a dark van pulled behind them, men exited the van and apprehended Max.

"Silvia," he yells, "run, they are after you as well, scream for the police, get to the American Embassy, call Mr. Giles."

"Max?"

"Run, now!"

She did, screaming for the police, the men pursued her until the police became involved, then they retreated to the van with Max. He was taken to a hotel, one floor was reserved for the visiting museum curator and his entourage of body guards. Max was tied to a chair and questioned by Klauss himself.

"You know who I am?"

He looked into the man's tormented face and eyes hardly recognizing him.

"You are the curator of the Museum Van Het Broodhuis in Brussels, Renee Klauss."

"Yes, and I met you several years ago on a trip there. Giles is in possession of a book on the occult that I gave him years ago. I know it kept him earthbound when he died. I want to possess it again so it can do for me as it did for him. Where is it Max?"

"He destroyed it, he told me." Max was being truthful.

"No, he couldn't, anyone who has read from its pages would die if it were destroyed."

Max then knew that Mr. Giles hadn't destroyed it.

"I called Giles earlier to bring the book if he wanted his son returned to him, he is coming but you won't be alive to rescue. I also told him how you would die . . . painfully with an I.V. of diluted snake venom."

"Why in God's name are you doing this?" startled at the man's cruelty.

"To punish him, you'll never see your wife again, your child won't have a father, Giles caused this."

Klauss left the room as they prepared the I.V. Max realized the man had lost his mind and couldn't be reasoned with. His mouth was taped to silence him.

Giles got the book, got packed and met Warren and Hector at the airport. Hector learned of Max's abduction from Silvia, he insisted on going. Mr. Giles had rented a private jet knowing Klauss would check the time of departure and arrival, someone else was ordered to take that jet as a small military jet was taken by Giles and the rescue team, the travel time would be cut in half. They had brought an arsenal of weapons aboard. Upon hearing from Klauss what was to be used to poison Max, Giles had contacted a herpetologist in Berlin for an anti-venom serum to counteract cobra venom. They would need it as soon as they reached Berlin a few hours later.

Once there, the serum was presented to Giles in the form of two shots and an I.V. The services of the herpetologist were well compensated. They arrived at the hotel, Giles walked in first, alone and was escorted to Klauss and handed him the book.

"Where is Max?" he asked as he looked at this sick tormented man.

"Don't waste time with formalities . . . and how am I? Sick and dying. Look at you Giles, young and healthy."

"Klauss, don't kill him."

"I imagine I already have even with your early arrival. Where are your friends?"

Giles didn't answer.

Hector and Warren were heavily armed and left their weapons outside in a rental car at a rear entrance. They then entered the hotel through the front entrance and rented a small suite on the fifth floor knowing that the fourth floor was restricted. They now dressed as hotel maintenance employees and retrieved their weapons which were inside two duffel bags in the small car parked at the employee entrance. A security guard at the entrance checked their I.D. and asked about the bags.

"Man, we are about an hour behind," Warren said. "Remove all our tools?"

"Do we look threatening?" Hector joked.

"Go on," the man said and laughed.

Once inside they entered the suite and unloaded their weapons and gear for leaving the hotel using a window if necessary. Then going with walkie-talkies to hear communication of hotel staff and their cell phones to communicate with each other, they began to knock on doors to be allowed in with a thermal imaging device citing they were looking for a faulty connection in the wiring under the floor. They were over the part of the fourth floor rented by Klauss. As they used the device over all areas of the floors they found Klauss, Giles and Klauss' entourage, they also found Max five rooms down the hall with two guards. Warren and Hector then split up. Hector then took the place of a hotel waiter delivering food, dressed appropriately he placed his armament under the cart and the two shots and I.V. for Max. He grabbed several desserts, hors d'oeuvres and anything appealing and turned toward the elevator right into the guard they passed coming into the rear entrance.

"Going somewhere Mr. Ramirez your security pass says?"

"You caught me, I was taking this food to my girlfriend upstairs, thought I wouldn't get caught. I am really maintenance."

"You're going to have to prove it, leave the cart here."

"But . . ."

"Let's go."

"At least allow me to . . ."

"Let's go now."

They left for the manager's office. Hector saw an opportunity because the office was off a small set of stairs isolated one-half floor up, no security cameras in the room. Within five minutes of meeting the manager he had subdued both men and using duct tape and a drug he had to anesthitize anyone if necessary, they presented no problem as he locked the office door and returned to the main floor. Now not able to find his cart he became frantic knowing Max was dying. He looked in every direction and finally spotted it still with the desserts on top parked in front of the kitchen. He quickly took it and made his way to the fourth floor, he saw guards and was questioned then fate stepped in as one of the guards watching Max stepped out of a room down the hall and signaled him to bring the food. Hector knew this was the right room from the thermal imaging.

"But this is going to someone else," Hector said to the man about the food. "I'm on the wrong floor."

"Come this way, we're hungry."

"Don't tell my boss, he'll be angry, I could use a good tip."

Hector came into the room with the cart, he didn't see Max at first, but knew he was there. He reached under the cart pulling out a gun with a silencer, shooting and killing both men. He locked the door then found Max, unhooked the I.V. giving Max a shot of the anti-venom and removed the restraints. He pulled him from the chair onto the floor then called Warren.

"Found him, administered the first shot."

"What shape?"

"Bad shape. I'm in over my head, will try to get us to the elevator, any help coming?"

"Not yet Hector. Giles is meeting with Klauss, I can't leave him."

"Understood."

"Got to go."

Hector was still wearing the outfit of the hotel staff, he was able to get through to Max as he placed him inside the cart. Then unlocking the door he rolled the cart past the first guard to the elevator.

"Bring more food." The man said.

Hector turned, "What sir shall I bring?"

"Anything, everything."

"As you wish, twenty minutes."

The elevator door opened, Hector rolled the cart in as another guard yelled out, "Stop him."

An old woman was on the elevator. "This is your floor," Hector said and pushed her out. The door closed then gunfire. Hector stopped the elevator between floors, pulled Max from the inside of the cart, he was barely conscious as Hector started him on an I.V.

"We wait," Hector told him. "The police have been called by now, it won't go well for us when they arrive and see us armed."

In the meantime Giles presented the book to Klauss. "We'll both read from it Klauss told Giles." They did. Warren was there.

"What are you asking from the Book?" Giles asked him.

"Naturally to live a long healthy life like yourself."

"I would have brought this book to you but you took my son and filled him with venom that is shutting down his organs, I promised the book something special if it would release Max and myself, to bring it the most cruel man I've ever known. It knows you as it knows anyone who has read from it, the Book has placed a part of itself in the three of us. The part of it in you has caused this terrible change because you are evil." Giles began speaking to the Book in Latin, he wasn't reading from it.

"What are you doing Giles?" Klauss asked nervously.

Suddenly something glowing comes out of the Book floating in a circle above them and touches Giles who tries to remain calm.

"Leave the others for me as well," the Book told him.

"Not the Sheriff or Hector."

"Agreed."

It pulls at Giles' chest removing itself from him and simultaneously does the same to Max in the elevator who groans in pain and passes out. Hector saw something but didn't know what it was. The Book now takes Klauss who is resigned to his fate and his entourage, several of which had fired into the elevator. They were gone in a matter of seconds.

Giles then asks the Book, "Where do you want to be placed?" The Book revealed that it wanted to be in the Metropolitan Museum in Houston. "I won't read from you again but I'm sure you'll enjoy that one," referring to Klauss.

The Book then closed and locked itself.

Warren wasn't believing what just happened. "Is it over?" he asked.

"If we can save Max it is."

They got Hector and Max and headed for the hospital emergency. Silvia was called and brought to the hospital.

"Why did it agree?" Warren asked Giles. "Why not take you?"

"Even with all the evil things I did under its influence I am a Christian. For that reason it couldn't totally turn me, I gave it what it wanted."

"The most cruel man you knew," Warren said.

"Sheriff I appreciate your efforts in this and you Hector. Whatever I can do for either one of you."

"Not necessary," Hector replied, "the baby should have its father, I grew up without one, it was tough."

"I imagine it would be."

Max, still in a German hospital was seen by the herpetologist as well as a team of very competent medical personnel. They didn't know how much damage had been done internally, time would tell. Silvia, Giles, Warren and Hector were there. She and Hector talked privately, Max remained in a coma, they sat close by. She conveyed her thanks to Hector realizing he had put himself at risk to save Max and Giles. They talked about the incident.

"I protected too much because at times I had to," Hector said.

"Hector, move to Houston with Max and me. Mother and Dad seem happy there in their new house, come be with us."

"Then who will protect them at the Camp? These veterans who are forgotten, some so messed up they take drugs to forget. The gangs have tried to force their way in, giving the young a purpose like a family would. I have to help them Silvia, no one else will."

Hector, the hardened soldier who had fought in Iraq, broke down.

"I haven't seen you like this Hector except . . ."

"When Dad passed away when I was ten. My place is with them at the Camp for now." He stood up, hugged her. "I hope he pulls through, let me know." She kissed him bye.

Giles, Silvia and Warren stayed after Hector was flown home. Three days later Warren then flew back to Houston concerned about the outcome.

Giles came to the room, as he did frequently, Silvia left for a short break.

"I know where you are Max it's safe there, no problems, no pain, only to those you've left behind. You encouraged me to fight, not to take the easy way out. You have an extra responsibility, Silvia and your unborn child, they need you, and we need you. Since we've tried everything to awaken you, I'll try a new approach, something irritating . . . Max, I'm afraid I must delay your meeting with your friends. Those calculations must be corrected before you leave . . . better yet just take the whole test over again, it would only put you two hours late."

Max stirred but didn't open his eyes as he spoke. "Rupert, Mr. Giles is keeping me late again to correct my calculations . . . where did I put my calculator?" Max reaches for it in his shirt pocket now realizing that he has no shirt on and is in a hospital bed. "Who are you?" he asks.

"Mr. Giles." He finds humor in Max's response.

"Take the entire test over again? I'm feeling disoriented."

"As you should. What do you remember?"

He thought for a few moments, "Being pushed into a van."

"And Silvia?"

"She was running away from me."

"Running from the men in the van, you told her to, she is safe."

"Tell me what happened."

"Do you recognize me? And no tests are needed, you are a doctor."

"You sound and act like Mr. Giles." Max hadn't fully recovered physically or mentally. "What happened?"

"Are you up to it?"

"I believe so."

"You remember Renee Klauss, museum curator in Brussels? You met him once on a trip with me, you were probably twenty-five, I considered him a friend. He gave me that book on the occult. He called days ago asking, demanding that I return the book to him, he was dying and realized that book had made it possible for me to remain earthbound when I died, he wanted the same second chance. I never destroyed the book for one reason, once I had read from it and you had found it on my desk and read from it, it knew us and there was a part of the book in both of us. Had I destroyed it, one or both of us would have died. I never realized that you or Silvia would be in danger if I didn't give him the Book. I told him it had been stolen from the Houston Metropolitan Museum rare books section. He called again and threatened to take the thing most precious to me and destroy it if I didn't return the book. Two days later he had you abducted, obviously having you followed."

"I am remembering parts of this."

"You were tied to a chair and given an I.V. of diluted cobra venom, you were never intended to survive. Hector Flores insisted on coming with the Sheriff and me. Hector rescued you."

"I seem to remember being in an elevator with him, bullets were being shot into a small opening as the doors were being forced open, we were stopped between floors. Then something was forced out of my chest."

"It happened to me simultaneously, the Book took itself out of us and took Klauss and his men, here we are now, safe."

"How forthcoming should I be with Silvia?"

"Perhaps not everything yet. She doesn't yet know I'm Mr. Giles." Silva came back from a break, stared at Max for a moment, "He's all yours." Giles hugged Max and Silvia then left. He called both Warren and Hector with the news. They left for home two days later. Silvia heard Mr. Giles talking to Max. She now understood what Max had been through and that Giles Fairlane was in reality Giles Macfarland.

Max couldn't forget the conversation between Hector and Silvia, "I couldn't respond but I heard you both, I have a plan that could help not only Hector but the Camp, Mr. Giles might come on board."

"Tell me," she said.

He discussed a possible medical center to be built on the land owned by the Camp. "Security, stores . . . who knows, a trade school teaching a variety of subjects."

"Max, when you dream you dream big," she kissed him.

"I always have, even as a child."

Weeks passed. Max had called Hector.

"Hello Hector, this is white ass."

He laughed. "Are you ever going to let me live that down?"

"Someday."

"How are you?"

"Better, glad to be alive, I want to thank you in person for what you did."

"Not necessary, but I'll be here."

"See you in about an hour."

He drove the hundred miles during the day to see the layout of the community and the surrounding land. Hector was working as a mechanic in the community. Max found him, he didn't know if Hector would be receptive.

"Good to see you Max." They shook hands.

"And you Hector, Silvia sends her love. I never got to thank you properly for the rescue, you put your life on the line. We had hoped you would join us and Silvia's parents in Houston."

"Here is where I feel most needed, most comfortable."

"There is something that could help people mend who have no place to go, these people you care for, looking out for them, protecting them . . . you do have a place to go, yet you have chosen to stay, that is to be commended. A medical center could be built for starters, then a good school to teach several trades say to those returning from the war, then a recreation center."

"We're all right Max, we'll fight our own battles within the community."

"You know what it's like to fight in a war, I haven't been in a war but I can see what war does to people as I work Sundays with Mr. Giles at the Free Clinic. So I have some understanding of their plight. Think about it, no charge to veterans, very small charge to the others, treating a variety of ailments, the equipment will be state-of-the-art. Mental issues of returning vets will also be addressed. The center built here would be large." Max then walks to his car.

"What would you call it?" Hector asked him as he followed.

"How does the Fogel-Flores Medical Center sound?"

"I'll have to think about that one."

Max left him hoping that Hector would accept his help at some point.

Later that evening at dinner Max brought up the subject to Mr. Giles. Marilyn and Silvia listened carefully.

"I want to discuss this with you Max, what the layout might look like, costs involved."

Max wasn't sure that Mr. Giles would go for the project but he owed Hector for saving his son and would keep an open mind to help in some way.

Since his capture and subsequent poisoning by Klauss, Max hadn't been sleeping well, finding any excuse to work at something. Silvia told Mr. Giles that Max seemed distant and nervous since the incident. Max heard a knock at his door, Silvia was downstairs. "Mr. Giles?"

"It's getting late but I wanted to see those drawings and hear your ideas."

Max showed him, explaining what might be possible, Mr. Giles was impressed. Max crossed the room to show him more information he had collected, he tripped over his own feet. "Didn't see that one coming." He yawned and got to his feet.

"Not sleeping well?"

"I don't seem to need as much sleep lately, where did I put those papers?"

"You have so many projects going lately, you could always deal with everything you had to do. The Free Clinic is one of the special projects we do together, we have to be one hundred percent when we are helping those people."

"Mr. Giles, what are you telling me?"

"Let's sit for a moment. I'm on board with this project but I won't be if this isn't resolved. You're nervous, distracted, not sleeping well, overloading your schedule till you can't do it all."

"I'm fine, just tired."

"I think I know you well enough to see that the events of four weeks ago have taken a toll on you."

"We got through it."

"But you didn't, not totally."

"I'm fine, really."

"You've been severely traumatized Max. You can't move on until you resolve this. I'm calling a friend tomorrow to help you through this."

"A therapist? No way."

"He has helped me through some rough patches, I trust him. It's bad enough that I caused this, what you went through."

"You mustn't blame yourself Mr. Giles." Max was being sincere.

"I do though, I want things to be right again, Silvia needs you, we need you. Try it this way Max, allow me to help you. The project will be our joint effort, it will happen."

Max said nothing but indicated he would cooperate. Mr. Giles left him something to help him sleep. Sleeping would bring back the events he didn't want to relive, but he would cooperate. Silvia walked into the room, they talked, and then he slept.

Max began therapy sessions, very careful to delete certain aspects of that event as the "Book" and would refer to Mr. Giles as his uncle, Giles Fairlane. The sessions would help him. Mr. Giles had only Max and sometimes Marilyn to confide in about certain things in his own past, as those victims in the mansion that he murdered as an earthbound spirit and taking the body of his murderer. The magnitude of these things and what he had done weighed heavily on him. He had seen that therapist as Giles Macfarland in the past regarding other matters.

It was Sunday three weeks after visiting with Hector. Hector pretended to be a patient at the Free Clinic. Max opened the door and seeing Hector as his patient was a surprise he hadn't expected.

"My chart said H. Flores," he said as he and Hector shook hands.

"Wanted to see for myself."

"I'll give you the grand tour, forty-five minute break, let's go." Max got another doctor to fill in during his absence if needed.

"I've been thinking about what you proposed for our Camp."

"Using your suggestions and the need involved in the Community, here are some possible scenarios." He showed Hector five different plans. "Mr. Giles is in on this."

Hector's eyes reflected his excitement without saying a word.

"When?" he asked.

"There are still legal matters to be solved but work should begin in a month, maybe sooner."

Hector stayed through the day watching the doctors and those patients down on their luck, many were veterans with various ailments treated here with respect. He had talked with those in the Camp to vote for the medical center and cooperation for the greater good, it was a tough sell.

A month went by, Silvia delivered a son a month early. Max was there by her side at the Giles Macfarland Hospital in Houston. They named him Giles Flores Fogel.

Mr. Giles and Max were on a campaign to solicit funding for the new medical center at the Camp. Someone very influential joined with them, Senator Marsdon who was a veteran himself and had faced problems upon returning from war. Hector then spoke, at times emotional, he was representing those in the Camp and their needs, he was willing to do anything to help. Others spoke with facts and figures ready. Everyone in the room was moved and voted in favor of funding the establishment of the Fogel-Flores Medical center as well as a learning center and recreational community center. Security would be stationed there 24/7 if the Camp became a town.

"Maybe someday," Hector said. "Thank you for everything."

Mr. Giles then told him, "No doubt it will be a town."

Sheriff Warren would be a consultant on the security aspect of the project.

CHAPTER XI

Tutor

Silvia and Max were adjusting to their new roles as parents. She had begun her nursing courses before the birth, on campus two days a week at Rice University, the other classes were by attending actual classes on-line in real time. Max was tutoring her, he also gave her tests. The C—he gave her on her last test caused her to be angry.

At dinner that evening with Mr. Giles and Marilyn she sat across from Max glaring at him.

"So Silvia," Marilyn asked, "how are your studies?"

Max looked at her and said nothing, he knew she was angry, he was frustrated. Mr. Giles and Marilyn felt the tension between them.

"Fine," she said, "certainly a challenge."

"Is Max doing a good job as tutor?" Mr. Giles asked.

"How does a C—sound?" she said.

No one said a word as Marilyn and Mr. Giles restrained themselves from laughing.

After dinner Max and Mr. Giles had a private talk as they often did. Silvia and Marilyn visited Little Giles upstairs.

"Are you sleeping?" Mr. Giles asked Max.

"Yes, much better, the therapist is about to cut me loose."

"And now you have a beautiful wife and son . . . not everything will go perfectly."

"You're telling me. I gave her a C—on a test yesterday."

"Did she deserve it?"

"Yes, however she is making A's generally in the course."

"Cut her some slack now and then, I did for you even while pushing you to excel. She is your student and your wife, patience and negotiation will play a big role in your lives. She will look to you for strength and guidance. Listen to her needs and advice, respect her as a partner."

"I think I'm doing that."

Mr. Giles gave him a pat on the shoulder, "Things will get better."

The next day Silvia began having doubts that she wanted to be a nurse.

"Silvia, where are you going? It's time to study," Max told her.

"I'm going to play tennis with Veronica, I need to get away from this."

He stood at the door of his study looking at her, "Have I said something to offend you besides giving you a C-?"

"I'm rethinking my decision to become a nurse, all this, the pressure, a child."

"Sit with me a moment."

She walked into the study, they talked.

"Have I been pushing you too hard? Mr. Giles gave you this scholarship. I wanted to but it was his gift to you, your dream. You don't want it anymore? If I'm pushing you away from this then I'll bow out, Mr. Giles could tutor you, he's tough but fair."

She looked at him, "I'm feeling pressured, we've been through some traumatic things, I almost lost you, learning things about . . ."

"The family?"

"It's all ok, I'm part of a wonderful family, different, married to a man I adore, I'm a mother, a college student, I don't know what's wrong Max."

"It's amazing when people, friends recognize the sacrifice and excitement of someone going back to school, they are envious and respect the commitment wishing they themselves were in school again. When Mr. Giles gave me my chance I would have done anything to be like him, now I think I am and wanted to help make your chance, your dream come true, but I won't push you away from it."

"Perhaps there is a way to schedule everything in."

"We did that for me, I got to take kickboxing, see my friends as I could, the occasional trip and study and now therapy," Max laughed as he said it.

"Let's see what a schedule might look like," she said.

"Sure?"

"I'll cancel tennis with Veronica. Can you tutor me now?"

The lesson was taught.

Veronica had earlier voiced concerns about Warren to both Silvia and Marilyn, that he was behaving differently. Giles and Max had been in touch but couldn't seem to meet with Warren due to his caseload.

That evening before dinner Max was taking a shower. Silvia surprises him as she joined him the shower, she touched his back softly.

"Fraternizing between students and teachers is strictly forbidden," he said as he turned to her, they kissed and made up.

An hour passed. Now realizing how late it was, both quickly dried. Now walking down the hall quickly he zipped her dress as she towel dried her wet hair and put it in a ponytail, she helped him with his shirt as he towel dried his hair and put it in a ponytail, then throwing the towel to the side on the floor. He fastened his belt, still walking quickly he tucked in his shirt. She walked backward in front of him zipping up his pants.

"Thank you Dear, not only would I have been embarrassed but Mr. Giles never tolerated being late or sloppy."

As they rounded the corner they saw Mr. Giles and Marilyn waiting. Everyone was dressed appropriately for the evening meal.

"My apologies," he said, "for being late. I kept my student overtime."

Giles and Marilyn noticed their hair, both in ponytails were wet. Max kissed Marilyn on the cheek and a pat to Mr. Giles' shoulder. Silva was now seated next to Max.

They were having a good time that evening. Later Max brought Little Giles downstairs for a visit as he quietly said, "I will be careful not to push her too hard, she was considering not getting her degree. We talked it out planning a schedule to include family, studies and tutoring as the priorities."

They then discussed the construction at the Camp.

Family was central to their lives and now Raoul and Ramirez would visit and occasionally sleep over at the mansion. Mr. and Mrs. Diaz and Hector with his companion Nicole would come for dinner when they could. Mr. Giles and Max discovered how much they liked grilling steak for their guests and being with their new extended family. Marilyn and Silvia were delighted and with the assistance of Mrs. Bradley they contributed special dishes to compliment the meals.

The next week Max called his trainer and Rupert to put kickboxing back into the schedule. His encounter with Klauss had affected his legs somewhat. Rupert and Max had sparred over the years, both were evenly matched.

CHAPTER XII

Sheriff's DNA

"I'm telling you Mr. Giles, something is wrong with the Sheriff." Max and Mr. Giles for weeks had tried to visit him. "Veronica has told Silvia that he is behaving differently."

"Then I'll just stop by unannounced, you're very intuitive."

Max arrived at the Bureau before Giles came to observe Warren. Giles then knocks on his door.

"Come in . . . Giles?"

"Thought I'd take a chance that you would see me. I haven't been successful setting up a time for lunch, wanted a tour."

"Come in, good to see you Giles." Warren had mixed feelings.

"The way I look now?"

"I won't ever get used to it, all of it seems like a dream."

"A bad dream, yet when I look at this face in the mirror and the long scar around my neck I am forced to remember the things I did, why I did them and have regrets about my decisions."

"There are Marilyn and Max, now Silvia and the baby."

Giles was sensitive where they were concerned. "Yes, the four people in the world I love the most. Max and I owe you more than a thanks for all you've done."

"What do you think of the Bureau?" Warren changed the subject.

"Impressive, I would like a tour if your schedule will allow it, then lunch, I'll treat."

"That's a deal." Warren swallowed some painkillers before they left. Giles made a call to Max. They began their tour. Warren appeared to be in pain.

Max entered his office unnoticed to find the names of the painkillers then gave Giles a call.

The restaurant was next. They talked about what transpired after the guests were freed from the Mansion, bringing Warren back, Max's marriage to Silvia and the baby.

"When are you and Marilyn getting married? You both love each other."

"I'm going to marry her, but so many projects are getting in the way."

"Don't blow it Giles."

"What about you and Veronica?"

Warren smiled, "I'm working on it."

"The offer still stands to help on cases if needed. We're still doing research but all three of us have experience in this field. We would be willing, no charge."

"A certainty Giles."

Warren left for a moment.

Mr. Giles put something in his wine.

Warren returned.

"I want to ask you something Sheriff, how have you been feeling since you were shot? Since you were brought back?"

"Not quite a year, seems longer. Honestly for the last five months I wished I hadn't been resurrected. There's an old saying, 'What's dead should stay dead'. Obviously restoring my life was a temporary thing."

Giles became defensive. "No, it was no temporary thing, you were given back a normal life span and because of that you found my murderer, saved lives, freed me. Why would you assume it was temporary?"

"Hold on Giles, I was grateful."

"Was? You aren't now?"

"Something happened, the doctors can't diagnose this. I haven't felt the same . . . chronic fatigue, pain."

"Is the pain level 1-10?"

"Tens. I'm still able to do my job. By the way, I don't require a date rape drug added to my wine."

"It was to render you willing to come with us for a thorough examination."

"I'll do you one better, come back with me to the Bureau."

Once they arrived Warren went to his office, removed the clip from his pistol and placed both along with his badge in his desk drawer, locked it, stood up, told his secretary he had a family emergency. "I'll let you know when I'll be back, four days probably." As he left with Giles, he placed his keys under his parked car. "Physically and emotionally I feel almost nothing, Veronica is beginning to think I'm avoiding her. I'll make this easy for you Giles, I'm asking you to undo what you and Max did."

"Are you telling me to end it? We can make this work, why end it?"

"Think about it, doing away with the only witness against you for murder. Who would believe a ghost took the body of his wife's lover, your murderer? Your fingerprints are altered, probably somehow your DNA."

"You're trying to provoke me into killing you and no the DNA can't be changed enough." Giles was driving faster now. They arrived at the mansion within an hour.

"See you've scaled down."

Giles was concerned. "It will be painful, we must reverse the entire process that brought you back."

Max was listening, he welcomed the Sheriff then had a private word with Mr. Giles.

"Where is Marilyn?" Warren asked.

"Probably with Veronica, shopping," he laughed.

Warren complimented the lavish furnishings.

"I was fortunate to retrieve these paintings as well as the furniture after I died."

Warren followed Giles to the basement laboratory.

"All right, if you're ready Max, the Sheriff is about to put his life in our hands so we may extinguish it. Remove your clothes Sheriff, no time to be modest."

Warren was hooked up to an I.V., Giles began to undo the life he had brought back over a year earlier. Warren was in intense pain but wouldn't cry out. A machine began to drain his essence away, Warren passed out.

"Mr. Giles?"

"Max, start the oxygen."

He and Giles studied the readings registering on a computer as a full body CT scan was done, the life signs were closely monitored. Warren was now at the point of death, a necessary step in diagnosing him. An epigenetic—DNA scope was then used.

"Max look at this."

"His DNA has fractures," he said in disbelief. "How, I cannot understand, was the process flawed? Yet the epigenome seems undisturbed."

After a few minutes of discussion he and Max agreed to use stem cells to repair his DNA as the best course of action.

"It seems the most logical."

They prepared stored cells and injected them into areas indicated by a machine. Marilyn watched unnoticed for a few moments.

"Now for one last injection."

"Sir?"

"A necessity." Giles saw Marilyn. "Hello my love."

"Why?" She asked as she looked at Warren.

"He presented a challenge, we answered, I'll tell you about it later, he should fully recover."

After an hour the machine used to direct and stimulate the stem cells was turned off. Hours would pass. Warren would remain at the residence as further tests were run.

"Do you still love him?" Giles asked.

"Not in the same way I love you, but yes."

"I was remembering something the Sheriff said at our lunch yesterday, don't let her get away, don't blow it. Have I blown it Marilyn with you?"

She kissed him, "You are the Giles I fell in love with, marry me."

This surprised him. "When?"

"As soon as possible. I'll call Veronica and tell her where he is."

Warren returned to work days later feeling more rested and alive.

Giles stopped by his office.

"I woke up four days later in my bed in my house with a beautiful woman by my side tending to me."

"Veronica is very caring where it concerns you," Mr. Giles told him.

"You changed your mind," Warren said, "why?"

"I never intended to take your life, you presented a challenge to Max and me, we had to meet it."

"What did you do to me?"

"Your DNA had fractures in it, you were dying, killing you was not an option, what caused it we can't ascertain."

A few moments passed.

"We're needed on a case," Warren said, "you interested?"

"When?"

"As soon as the FBI briefs us, it's their case, they need two pathology forensics experts."

"We're in."

CHAPTER XIII

Giles and Marilyn Marry

The mansion became the place for a second wedding, there were around fifty guests. Max assisted Mr. Giles and was his best man. Veronica and Silvia assisted Marilyn and Veronica was her maid of honor.

"You seem very calm Mr. Giles," Max said.

"I assure you I'm not, only pretending. Technically I'm married to her."

"We can't count that."

"No, I suppose not."

"It seems logical since you both love each other to take the next step."

Giles smiled as he stood up and took another look in the mirror. "This is it," he said. He wore a dark brown suit and vest.

They walked to the large room adjoining the parlor to await the bride.

Warren sat with the guests. Veronica was dressed in a yellow silk knee length dress. Marilyn entered to the theme song 'I Will Always Love You' sung by a soloist accompanied by violin. She wore a beige silk knee length Versace dress with baby's breath in her hair. Giles had assumed that Marilyn could never love him like she did before the transformation. She did, now that he truly was Giles again. They had both matured in their love. He had risked everything to come back to her and to Max. The scar across his neck was a reminder to Marilyn of what he'd gone through. They said their vows before the priest. Max's excitement was tempered with emotion which he concealed as he watched the man he admired most marry Marilyn again.

"Now I present to you Mr. and Mrs. Giles Fairlane, you may now kiss the bride," the priest said.

Giles whispered, "Just wait until the guests leave."

Marilyn then whispered something to him.

"Everyone, down the hall, we're only beginning to celebrate," Giles said.

They celebrated through the evening. There was a staff of extra help serving the guests, a chamber orchestra provided the music. Max had coordinated the events for the wedding. He and Silvia were caught up in the excitement.

"Glad you could come Sheriff," he said.

"Wouldn't have missed it, especially with a beautiful escort."

The evening went on then one by one the guests left. Giles and Marilyn went upstairs. He loved her deeply, he knew he could totally love her without hesitation.

CHAPTER XIV

The Cartel

Hector had met Nicole Matthews, a nurse at the Free Clinic, when he visited Max earlier. They started dating soon after. He wouldn't bring her to the Camp not wanting to show his humble circumstances and not wanting to frighten her even though she dealt with all kinds of people, mostly those down on their luck. She had enormous respect for the deceased Giles Macfarland and now his stepbrother Giles Fairlane, not realizing he was in fact Giles Macfarland and respect for Max Fogel.

Activity at the Camp was progressing where the buildings were concerned, three main structures. Illegal activities were also present. Hector and Max were viewing the progress one afternoon when four men, newcomers in the Camp, confronted and threatened Hector, he had an earlier encounter with two of them, it had escalated into a fight. He had been warned by some of the residents of gang activity escalating and rumors of a Cartel takeover. One of the older veterans living there, pretending to be drunk got close enough to hear these men planning an attack on the Camp that evening essentially taking over to funnel drugs from the Cartel. Hector and Max with this information paid a visit to Sheriff Warren and identified all four suspects. Warren found them on the Bureau Criminal Database.

"Bad news Hector," he said as Hector's suspicions proved true. "The Mexican Cartel probably saw a golden opportunity at the Camp especially recruiting gang bangers. You need security out there and I'm working on it, it's frustrating the red tape involved in this."

"The funding hasn't come through for the security from the Committee due to the legal issues involved," Max said.

"I know you're both trying. I don't know how far legally I can go to stop them, there's no 911 to call," Hector told them.

"If it's kill or be killed do what you have to . . . how many others to help you?" Warren asked.

"Not enough. Something is about to happen and we're not prepared."

Warren was sympathetic. "I'm sending two of my men, our manpower and budget are stretched but for as long as we can they'll stay out there until something else can be done."

"Mr. Giles and I will pay for their time."

"Sounds like a plan Max."

"Thanks," Hector said.

"Do you carry a gun?" Warren asked Hector.

"I do."

"Watch your back, here's my cell number. Someone you trust might be compromised. The deputies will get there tonight, I'll be there as well."

"If only to treat the wounded," Max said, "I'll be there after I retrieve supplies from the Clinic and head your way. I need a place to put the wounded, sheets, towels, any alcohol, liquor as an anesthetic and to sterilize if my supplies run out."

"Will do, see you both later."

Warren stayed behind as Hector and Max left, he made a call then walked over to his lieutenant.

"Any plans for the evening Dawson?" he asked him."

"No Sir."

"Clock out and come with me, we're going to stop the Cartel."

They both brought an assortment of guns, rifles, night vision equipment and several two-foot long one inch wide steel pipes. They now stopped by an adjoining detention center. Warren got six prisoners and took them to another room where Dawson was waiting.

"If you want to fight, maim and possibly kill, come with us."

"Sir?" Dawson asked looking at these huge men.

He then explained, "There is a place called the Camp an hours drive. The Mexican Cartel is making a big move tonight to take over this small community made up of people that are the most vulnerable, veterans, single mothers, kids, most live below the poverty line. Your only weapons will be your fists and these two-foot steel pipes to use as you see fit. Let's be there and spoil their assault on these folks. Try and not harm the general population there."

"What do we get out of this?" One asked him, the largest and most tattooed of these big men.

"Maybe you're killed, maybe my lieutenant and I are killed. If we make it, I'm recommending leniency in your sentences for defending at the risk of your own lives these people . . . all of you are headed for lengthy prison terms. There is a doctor stationed there, a friend. If you are wounded he will be close by probably in the barn . . . now who's coming with us?"

All six followed. Warren signed them out, their orange uniforms would set them apart. He was questioned why he was removing these men from custody.

"I need them for a project for a few hours."

They left in a van.

Hector and the two deputies had alerted several in the Camp. Warren and the others arrived.

"Max is in the barn setting up a triage of sorts," Hector told him as he watched the big men getting out of the van.

Warren stepped inside. "Ready?" he asked Max.

"Ready as I'll ever be."

Max then called Mr. Giles to tell him what was going on. As worried as he was he didn't chide Max for being secretive even telling Mr. Giles not to come. "Sheriff Warren is here with the cavalry so-to-speak, it's starting."

"Be careful Max, all of you be careful."

Gunfire was heard as the Cartel began moving through the Camp. One of the deputies was shot then was moved to the barn. Max began to work on his first casualty. Several of the residents, mostly the women with small children had taken refuge in the barn and assisted Max as needed. The sound of generators was heard giving light for surgery. More gunfire, two of the residents were wounded and quickly brought to the barn. The Cartel wasn't expecting resistance. As Max was removing the bullet from the deputy someone opened the door and pointed a gun directly at him. The man who entered was young and said in Spanish that he was part of the Cartel. Max replied in Spanish that he and his patients were no threat. He had the deputy drinking vodka to numb the pain.

"Stop," the man said, "or I'll kill you."

"Don't save his life?" Max continued now to suture the wound.

"I'll kill you," he said again.

"Then do what you must." Max was nervous but pretended otherwise.

The young man aimed the gun to fire as someone else entered the barn and beat the man with a large steel pipe until he was unconscious. Max and the others were startled to see this huge man in an orange uniform, arms covered with tattoos.

"Thanks," Max told him.

The man left saying nothing, only gave a nod.

Several more were brought in wounded. Blood was needed. Max made an announcement in Spanish and English, "We desperately need blood, only those who don't have a disease and know their blood type can give blood." Several lined up to give.

Hector made use of his street fighting and karate training on the Cartel, he also carried a gun and a sizeable knife.

Warren and the two remaining deputies split up, one was then stationed at the barn. The six 'big guys' as they were called startled even the calloused Cartel with their fighting abilities, they had killed or put several out of commission. The residents used what they needed to defend themselves, several had guns and knives. The lights surrounding the new construction were now turned off by the Cartel, they had planned to burn down the buildings. More gunfire. Warren was grazed by a bullet. Max stopped the bleeding using bandages. One of the large men had been stabbed in the leg.

"Drink this," Max instructed him. The alcohol calmed and numbed the patient. "An artery," he said as he gave the man a shot. One of those in the barn had been a nurse and assisted as Max operated. The other five 'big guys' went with Warren to weed out the remaining Cartel and gangbangers even as they had also sustained injuries. These weapons they confiscated became theirs, very disconcerting to Warren and the deputies. Warren knew from an informant that the Cartel was preparing to burn the new buildings as soon as possible.

Hector came to Max, a stab wound to the hand and bruising from a fight.

"Take a number," Max said and laughed nervously.

"It's busy here."

"You aren't kidding, who's winning anyway?"

"I think we are." Max got to Hector as soon as possible, five sutures later.

It was four hours into the fight, still gunfire, yelling and screaming. Another deputy was hit and brought into the barn.

"A bullet to the abdomen, drink this," he told the deputy handing him a swallow of vodka, then he administered a shot and began to operate. There were more volunteers assisting and giving blood for transfusions.

"Will he pull through?" Warren asked as he stood by for a few moments.

"He should."

"We'll be on the roof," he said then left.

Max sat exhausted after the operation, his clothes and shoes were bloodied from the patients he treated. Then there was the sound of cars, all hoped it wasn't the Cartel but it was. Warren, Dawson and four others stood on the unfinished medical building and two on each of the other buildings using the night vision equipment and firing with the intent to wound or kill anyone that came near the project with intentions of destroying the buildings. There were sounds of yelling and anguish, the noise of guns, more wounded as homemade explosives and more sophisticated explosive devices detonated too quickly killing several of the Cartel. An assault was launched on the barn shooting at random in hopes of killing the wounded and the innocents inside. Everyone's nerves were strained to the breaking point but they tried to stay as calm as possible, several now assisting the wounded. The one nurse took a towel and water and wiped the blood from Max's face as he continued operating. Twenty-six patients were saved. Thread became very important as supplies dwindled, four in the barn had been suturing small wounds.

Two more hours passed. Max fell asleep exhausted. Then more cars, trucks, helicopters above.

"Max . . . wake up," Hector said as he entered the barn. "Help has arrived."

Max stood up.

"It's the National Guard," another said outside.

Troops went everywhere. Warren advised them of the activities that had transpired.

"The 'big guys' in the orange uniforms are in my custody, they fought the Cartel and might be carrying weapons confiscated during the fight. There are the wounded and a doctor in the barn. Who sent you boys?"

"Senator Marsdon, when he got word of this called the Governor who sent us."

There was still gunfire and resistance. Max was glad to see that medical personnel had come as well.

"There are twenty-two in here now who needed doctoring, some left continuing to fight after being wounded . . . less critical. Several are still critical, more injured will be found. Those who fired at the barn were hoping to injure or kill more."

He was praised for tirelessly helping the wounded even for the ones he couldn't save. He called Mr. Giles.

"Help arrived."

"Senator Marsdon had the Governor send them ASAP."

"You called him?"

"Yes."

"Thank God."

"You must be exhausted."

"I never thought this many, not everyone made it, several in the barn assisted me."

"When are you coming back?"

"Not tonight, tomorrow when those are evaluated and the most critical evacuated then I'll be home."

"Rest if you can, I'm proud of you Max."

"I have much to tell you . . . and Silvia?"

"Worried but fine. I'll tell her."

The National Guard stayed, the patients were stabilized and the more seriously wounded were taken to hospitals in Houston and the Free Clinic for the less severe injuries at no cost.

Warren and Dawson then found the 'big guys', they surrendered their weapons collected during the fight, all but one.

"I won't," he said, "I won't go back there."

"You fought bravely," Warren told him, "give me a chance to help you, don't make this turn ugly."

"I'm looking at thirty years to life."

"No one wins if you die."

After several tense minutes of negotiation the man finally surrendered to Warren. They then left for the Bureau with the 'big guys' in tow. All injuries sustained would be addressed in the Bureau Prison Hospital.

Max headed for home knowing that several of the National Guard and two deputies would remain at the Camp until further notice. When he reached home Mr. Giles was outside waiting. He hugged Max and helped him with the medical equipment to be returned to the Clinic. Then he saw where bullets had hit Max's car but said nothing about it.

Max was too exhausted to be carrying on a conversation. Once inside, Silvia hugged and kissed him but didn't press him for answers. Marilyn also gave him a hug.

Max removed his bloodied shoes and clothes and stood in the warm water of the shower for several minutes allowing the water to wash the blood off. Silvia made him sit as she washed his hair and scrubbed his back, he couldn't.

The next morning he stirred when Silvia touched his back, he turned to her.

"What's going on pretty girl?"

They kissed.

"You hungry?" she asked.

"What time is it?"

"Eleven."

"I'm hungry."

They went to the kitchen and had breakfast.

"Tell me if you feel like talking about it."

"It was a war, the Cartel was moving in and going to take the property with the help of gangbangers then funnel their drugs from there to Houston. It was incredible."

"I heard you were pretty incredible yourself."

"They had all the action outside while I was in the barn playing doctor." Max said this to be humorous.

"They needed a doctor, you were there, Hector said so."

"Those guys kept fighting, then more Cartel, more gunfire then the National Guard. I tell you Silvia I never experienced anything like that, never want to again."

"What about the man who threatened to kill you?"

"One of the Sheriff's prisoners who fought with us stopped him fortunately."

"Fortunately, you were in danger."

"Things turned out all right." Max was surprised that she knew. Silva began to cry, Max held her.

Mr. Giles and Marilyn walked in. "Can we join you?" Mr. Giles asked.

"Certainly," Max told them.

They discussed the events of the last two days.

"Plans are now moving quickly to make the Camp a town," Giles said, "then police, 911."

"We came so close to losing this one."

"But we didn't."

"The people there are to be commended, they fought to preserve the first ray of hope they've had in years . . . those buildings, a future for them and their children."

"On a lighter note what about your car?" Giles asked.

"The bullet holes are all in one direction, close together, I'll ask Hector."

He did. Hector made chrome rings around each hole giving the car a unique look.

CHAPTER XV

Warren & Veronica—Hector & Nicole

Warren was commended for his quick action to save the Camp and its residents. He had testified as to his actions and those of his deputies. He asked that the 'big guys' be given consideration for lighter sentences. All of them on the Sheriff's advice asked to eventually live at the Camp and help protect it. Max and Hector as well as several of the residents at the Camp testified in favor of the Sheriff and those deputies who came with him. The six 'big guys' as they were called appeared in the Houston Chronicle and several other newspapers and T.V. media along with Warren and his men. Public opinion went in favor of those who fought the Cartel. As the trials of each of the 'six' approached the Governor stepped in giving each reduced sentences to be served at the Camp, living there as residents and protectors. All would wear ankle monitoring devices for a time. Each man was in agreement with this arrangement. It meant a new beginning.

Hector was recognized as the leader there. Everyone assisted the 'big guys' and the deputies to get settled in, this before a police presence would be there permanently.

The Camp was put on the fast track to become a town which it did months later, the name would be Camp Veracruz as named by the residents. The buildings were taking shape. Those who fought to preserve the Camp as well as every resident, the committee that poured money into it, Senator Marsdon and others were given a grand tour of the three buildings. Everyone living there was experiencing change, change for the better.

Warren and Veronica got together as often as they could, Warren's schedule was demanding but he wouldn't lose her, they had grown close.

She as a real estate broker was doing very well. She admired him, he was fascinated by her. She never knew that Giles Fairlane was Giles Macfarland, neither Warren nor Marilyn divulged that secret. On rare occasions Warren asked Giles and Max to help on certain cases involving forensics he told her.

Hector hadn't told Nicole where he lived. One night in Houston he took her to an upscale restaurant. Max advised him to be forthcoming.

"By not telling Silvia everything I hurt her deeply, I almost lost her."

Hector took his advice. Nicole asked where he lived.

"We know so little about each other," Hector said. "Where I live is a community south of Houston called the Camp. When I returned from the Iraq war I settled there, I had family living there. Most of the residents are poor, veterans with no place to go, damaged mentally and physically, families with little or no medical help. I have dedicated myself to protecting these vulnerable people, gangbangers keep trying to infect the young ones. The Mexican Cartel tried to take over the Camp and there was a war, you might have read about it, they pushed, we pushed back with guns and anything to fight with. There were injuries."

"I read about it and the coverage on the evening news," Nicole replied startled that Hector had been there. "I think you're very brave."

"This information has probably turned you off."

"Off? Of you? Not really."

"Don't feel sorry for me?"

"No, I find you very attractive, you care about people."

"I work as a mechanic, I understand machinery. When the Camp becomes a town I'll open my own shop . . . 'Hector's', can fix anything." He laughed. "What are your goals, your dreams Nicole?"

She drank her wine then, "To keep working at the Free Clinic, since I'm a nurse I'll stay in the medical field. I want to be with someone who loves me, who will make a good husband and father to our children, to explore life together. Talk about telling too much, have I turned you off?"

He smiled, "No you haven't." He drank his wine.

"Dinner was wonderful," she said.

He looked at her blue eyes and auburn hair and wanted to kiss her, then he did.

"Weren't you on U-Tube recently fighting someone who looks a lot like Dr. Fogel?"

Hector tried to lie his way out of it. "I get that all the time, wasn't me."

He kissed her again.

CHAPTER XVI

Doctors Without Borders—Rescue

Mr. Giles had heard the news about a group of doctors, members of the Doctors Without Borders being attacked by a militia of gunmen in Bolivia. The group was led by a friend Dr. Bolivar, a distant relative of the country's namesake. All were assumed killed or captured. Mr. Giles relates this news to Max and about the plea of the families on CNN news to not harm the captives. Dr. Bolivar's wife was very desperate in her plea, Giles was moved but didn't call her.

"Who would I say was calling her?" he told Max. "Giles Macfarland doesn't exist now, not to her."

"What are you thinking Mr. Giles? You want to find him?" Max asked.

"Something is telling me I could find him."

"You and what army?"

"With money I can buy an army, a sizeable one."

Max just sat down, he knew Mr. Giles and there was no way to talk him out of his resolve when he was so moved to do something.

"Then I'll go with you."

"That means a lot to me but I leave the girls and Little Giles in your care until I return."

"Absolutely I am participating in finding the doctor, you'll need all the help you can get and moral support."

"Max . . ."

"No, I'm not staying here while you put yourself at risk. Marilyn, Silvia and Little Giles will have people here looking after them. We should be forthcoming with them about your plan."

"I wish you'd reconsider Max," Giles was sincere.

"We should call the Sheriff and get his advice on this."

"Agreed." Giles wasn't happy dragging Max into this.

Marilyn and Silvia weren't taking this latest news well. Both argued with their husbands against going, about the dangers there to no avail.

"Strong willed," Marilyn said. "If they are together they have a better chance of survival and if Warren joins them it's making the odds the best they can be," Marilyn told her.

"How do you deal with this when those we love put themselves in danger?"

"Trying to be positive and believe that they will succeed. Sometimes I think the three of them are trying to save the world, and trying to talk them out of it proves to be very difficult."

Giles had spoken to Warren for advice.

"What are you two planning besides getting yourselves killed?"

Giles related the story of his friend Dr. Bolivar. "Whether it is a rescue or a burial we must find him and the others."

"This army you're planning to hire, allow me to pick the men. I'll get you the best and join you in the search. I know a few things about search and rescue."

"Your efforts to help us are greatly appreciated," Mr. Giles said.

"We leave in five days for Bolivia, is this agreeable?" Warren asked.

Mr. Giles looked at Max, he gave a nod, "Yes agreed."

"Max, any ideas?"

"One, a crash course in doctoring for you Sheriff and I probably should update my will."

Warren agreed on both knowing the danger of this mission.

They left on a military transport plane. Warren selected a Colonel Blake that he served with in Afghanistan to command the twenty Special Ops. Warren would pose as an intern training with Giles and Max. He had learned several medical terms and had a few hours of hands on experience.

They arrived several hours later in Bolivia at a small airstrip. The three were driven to a certain point then the guide left them as planned to continue on foot to find the militia camp and allow themselves to be captured, Warren advised Max and Giles, each knew the code word to bring the Special Ops forces in for a rescue. Giles was now regretting his decision to put everyone in jeopardy, he told Max.

"Mr. Giles let's try to think positively about this, we're here, we will find the doctors, hopefully alive."

Giles gave a firm pat to his shoulder, "For the encouragement."

Warren had misgivings about the mission from the beginning. He didn't share this with Giles or Max.

Two hours later they walked into the camp followed by gunmen. The inhabitants and their children stared at these strangers. They were brought before a man they assumed was the commander.

"Do you speak Spanish?" he asked angrily.

"Yes and English," Warren replied.

"Are you spies?"

"No sir, we were attempting to join our friends, if we can find them, doctors from the Reed Clinic to offer medical assistance in the jungle hospitals. Our guide was killed in a fall."

"That one," pointing to Warren, "is in training," Max told him.

"You three will be tested. Remove your shoes. Take them," he told an aide and pointing to Max, "put him near the woman."

All three were now to listen for any information concerning the missing doctors. The army hired by Giles was totally concealed, monitoring the activity there and looking for the missing doctors, hearing and analyzing every conversation, thermal imaging was also used as possible within the dense jungle.

Max talked to the woman prisoner who was a nurse, tethered by a long chain to a nearby tree. He was tied to another tree and forced to sit on the ground. Giles and Warren were each tied to trees some distance away. Max began to ask the woman questions. She was tan, beautiful and tall, had a long scar on her left cheek, medium length dark curly hair. He spoke in both English and Spanish.

"We are looking for Dr. Bolivar and his colleagues."

"I know English," she said. "I am a nurse, I wasn't with the recent group that was killed. I am a prisoner here, I'm Niah."

"Were they all killed?"

"I don't know, I don't know your name."

"Dr. Fogel . . . Max."

"We don't wear shoes, sometimes we can wear thong sandals. Tell me about your friends."

Max took a liking to her, she seemed to have a positive attitude about her incarceration.

"Dr. Warren is an intern, Dr. Fairlane is head of our group, a very capable surgeon, I am also a surgeon. Doctors Without Borders is the organization we represent."

"From what country?"

"America . . . so how long have you been here?"

"Several months, working at anything, some nursing as needed. I was separated from my group and was kidnapped."

"Is that man the leader here?"

"Yes, and he can be brutal."

Just then the Commander made his rounds looking at the prisoners striking Max and pulling Niah's hair. Both Warren and Giles also received punishment. He yelled and was antagonistic toward his prisoners. He then left them. Evening was approaching, the jungle was damp and stiffeling, mosquitoes were unrelenting. All pertinent vaccines had been given to all the men who had travelled there.

"Are they planning to feed us Niah?"

"Probably tomorrow . . . hang in there, tomorrow will come soon."

Hours later, Max was awakened by someone touching him.

"What are you doing?" he asked, startled.

"Quiet," a woman's voice told him in a whisper. It was dark.

"I . . ."

"If you make another sound I will harm the woman and then your two friends." She then proceeded to violate him. He felt anger in her touch. Nothing more was said, she left him several minutes later.

The next morning he looked over to see the female prisoner that she was all right. He said nothing to her about the incident. They were fed then taken to either save the wounded or do manual labor in the camp. They were not allowed to see any of the captured group they came to find or know if any survived. Niah studied them as did the man known as militia commander. She assisted Max as did Warren on a patient. She attempted to give a certain drug to the patient, Max saw her about to make a fatal mistake.

"No, you'll be killing him," he said as he took the syringe from her. "Dr. Warren tie off the wound here." He did so. "Administer one cc penicillin."

Warren made it in one try.

"Here, start on this patient," the Commander told Warren.

"But I need him here," Max told him.

The Commander grew angry.

"Because he is my student, allow me to watch him evaluate the next patient."

He nodded his OK.

Max and Warren then discussed the procedure. It was a serious injury but not fatal.

"I leave you to it, if you have a problem . . ."

Max and Niah then operated on the first patient. They finished an hour later then he checked on Warren who had removed a bullet and sutured the wound. He gave his ok.

Giles was then called in to repair a broken leg. Niah assisted him. Max and Warren were then sent back to do manual labor in the camp, moving debris, stones, branches, making repairs to the barracks.

Later Giles finished and was sent to join Max and Warren who discussed Max's night visitor.

"Giles and I had an encounter with someone checking us out."

"How far did it go?" Max asked.

"Far. It was a woman."

Giles just shook his head, disgusted with the whole incident.

"Everyone remember the code if things go south," Warren said.

"Are we being monitored constantly?" Max asked.

"Yes."

All were tired, the jungle was hot and humid. Niah became convinced that they were doctors.

Max continued conversing with Niah.

"You'll get used to the heat, the humidity is another matter." She had earlier told him that she was from Mexico, her husband had died and had no children and now she asked Max about himself.

"Not much to tell. I emigrated from Germany at seventeen, my parents were dead, I was adopted, put through school, met my wife Silvia, we have a son, and I adore them and miss them terribly."

"Maybe there will be a rescue soon. We'll all be fed tonight."

That night after being secured by the guards, Max fell asleep and the prisoner Niah nearby. He was again awakened by the same visitor, a woman. She began her assault on him again. He could hear the sound of a large knife being laid beside him.

He whispered to her, "I would feel less threatened if you placed that formidable knife somewhere else."

She didn't reply as she moved the knife. He faced another night of torment at her hands.

The next day Niah called to him, "Max, wake up, they'll be coming soon, you look exhausted."

"I haven't been sleeping well."

"You'll adjust," she said.

"Did you hear anything last night, see anyone?"

"No."

The Commander came with his men to put the doctors to work. Max had a pregnancy to contend with, complications of bleeding which he managed to stop. The militia had a stockpile of medicines which the doctors could choose from, even a refrigeration unit was available for some medications. Giles doctored two men, victims of snakebite. Warren doctored cuts and bruises. Niah assisted all three.

After several hours of doctoring members of the militia, they were allowed to eat. Max at first refused. It wasn't what he was being fed but the way in which they were treated as prisoners.

"Eat it Max," Niah told him, "don't expect American tastes to be satisfied here." She knew it wasn't about the food.

He reluctantly ate.

Later Max, Giles and Warren joined another prisoner to fix a water pump by a small lake. The prisoner knew how to fix the pump and used the three to help. Tools were brought for the job which took several hours. One of the guards remained with the men while the other took a break relieving himself. An argument started between the guard and the prisoner, the guard hit him, the prisoner went ballistic insulting the guard and stabbing him with a screwdriver. He then threw the guard in the water and ran for the jungle. Warren jumped in after the guard to save him. Max and Giles lifted him onto a small dock. Just then the other guard approached, shouting at them, they had the man's blood on them, the screwdriver left behind was incriminating. He motioned for them to return to camp carrying the body.

The Commander demanded that they be put in a prison. He discussed this with another in the barracks.

"Certainly if they did this the punishment will be severe, if they are telling the truth then we must capture the prisoner who escaped, they don't seem capable of this."

"Then how do you want to proceed?" the Commander asked.

"Let me handle it, chain them as before, find the other one."

They were chained again to the same trees.

Max saw Niah again he was distressed.

"What happened?" she asked.

"You wouldn't believe me."

"Max tell me, try to relax and start at the beginning."

He related the events of helping another prisoner fix the pump at the lake. "We were finished when one of the guards began to argue with the prisoner, I don't know his name, the prisoner insulted the guard and stabbed him with a screwdriver, pushed him in the water and ran in the direction of the jungle, the other guard had gone somewhere, when he came back, Dr. Warren had pulled him out of the water, we pulled him onto the dock, covered in his blood . . . we couldn't save him."

"The penalty for murder here is severe," she said.

"How do we prove our innocence, why should anyone believe us?"

"I believe you," she said as she studied his face and behavior.

He knew he could say the Special Ops code and end this but he waited hoping for a miracle—time to find the other doctors. He needed Niah and knew she cared.

Special Ops heard all of this and began a search for the criminal. The three weren't fed that evening. Niah had been taken for nursing duties. Returning in an hour she brought Max some bread which she quickly fed him before she was again chained. Night approached and so did the night visitor.

"Calm yourself," she whispered to him.

Max said nothing and again reluctantly submitted to her.

The next day Niah was taken to work in the field. Max was taken to join Warren and Giles in a pre-trial for the crime of murder. They got to talk briefly as they walked to the small building.

"Anything Max?" Warren asked.

"No. I have been talking to Niah gathering some information but nothing to lead us to the hostages."

"Keep trying," Giles said concerned about Max and their fate if found guilty. Is your night visitor still . . . ?"

"Oh yes, getting more aggressive with every visit."

"Do you feel threatened by her enough to end this?" Giles asked.

"This trial concerns me more, hold off on ending it," Max said.

They were taken inside a small building. The Commander pointed to the three and read the charges against them. "Worthy of death or torture," he said.

A man was selected to represent them. Each one gave his testimony as the man questioned each. After two grueling hours of this, they were taken to a small cage where a man was being held.

"The prisoner!" Warren said in disbelief.

Special Ops had found him and shot him with a tranquilizing dart. He was moved in the direction of the Commander's approaching men who had been searching for him. The three were then made to sit as judgment was pronounced on the man. He was taken from the cage cursing as he was literally hacked repeatedly with a machete until he died.

"Punishment has been carried out," the Commander said. "Back to work."

They did work while mentally carrying the images of this brutal execution, painting a newly refurbished barracks, cleaning hedges and branches. Later they were doctoring. All three were then ordered to bathe and shave.

"What's the occasion?" Warren asked as he heard music.

"A wedding festival," a soldier replied.

Niah was there. All the prisoners were sitting on a bench chained.

"I'm glad for you Max," Niah said, "and your friends."

"I feel relieved and to be clean shaven again and a bath." He laughed.

Warren and Giles were feeling lucky to be alive.

"What now?" Giles asked.

"Probably tomorrow, we've overstayed our welcome."

The evening was festive and a way to release the tensions, American beer and Bolivian wine were served with a feast. There was laughter. Finally hours later the celebration drew to a close. Everyone was taken to their areas where they were chained for the night. Niah had been taken earlier and chained before Max arrived.

The night was damp and warm as usual. Mosquitoes, the usual pests, were rampant.

"This must be hell to you Niah."

"After several months I am almost used to it . . . the night was special."

"Yes it was."

"Goodnight Max."

"And to you Niah."

Hours later Max was awakened again by the woman visitor.

"Why?" he asked her.

She didn't answer as she began to violate him. Several minutes went by, then as she was about to leave, "Because I love you."

He was confused but said nothing more fearing for Niah's safety.

Morning came. Max saw that Niah was safe. He was feeling physical pain and nausea. Niah observed him and he seemed non-responsive to her greeting. He, Giles, Warren and Niah were to do work detail first while awaiting those needing medical attention. Suddenly he falls to the ground. Giles and Warren attempt to help but are pushed away and told to keep working by a subordinate to the Commander. The Commander hears the commotion and arrives, taking his machete from its sheath he is threatening Max, suddenly Niah gives a subtle signal to the Commander to not harm Max and points in the direction of a tent. Warren sees this.

"Giles, Niah just gave a signal to the Commander and he obeyed, she is the Commander and he is her general."

"The woman prisoner?"

"I'm telling you what I saw."

Just then several came for help having been stung by scorpions. Giles and Warren were also stung while helping them. They were given a salve for their wounds and instructed to dispense it to other victims as well as applying it as necessary. Niah is checking Max who had passed out, with the help of an aide she literally checked him from head to toe for stings applying the salve and administering a shot for severe infection. She returned to assist Warren and Giles having no idea that her true identity had been discovered. The shots were only for the severely infected, some sores were lanced.

"These scorpions have migrated south for the last month, they should leave this area within two or three days," she told them.

"Why this migration?" Warren asked her.

"The water forces them south. They are at times a deadly species."

"Niah, have you seen Max?" Giles asked.

"Yes, the Commander is dealing with him, he had a severe infection . . . nausea and exhaustion are two of the more common symptoms of the scorpion's sting."

"Have you ever been stung in the months you've been here?"

"Several times, I had my arm lanced and nausea followed."

That evening every patient had been tended to. Niah returned to the tent where Max was, she stayed with him through the night. She was in love with him, she knew what it meant to be close to someone, it didn't end well. While he was sleeping restlessly, she began to love him, kissing and caressing him, she talked to him.

It was now morning, he woke up and saw her sitting by his cot asleep.

"Niah?"

She woke up. "How are you feeling?"

"Is this question from Niah the prisoner or Niah the Commander?"

"When did you . . . ?"

"Things didn't quite fit together and there was the angry night visitor. I didn't know if I was meant to survive it."

"The village was attacked by scorpions, you had an infection from the stings."

"You saved my life."

"Yes. Your friends survived the stings, nothing severe. If you're feeling strong enough I want to take you somewhere today."

Max got up, though weakened he would go with her. He dressed. An aide was close by as she took Max to a clearing in the jungle. They sat as she talked to him.

"I come here for tranquility and peace. The deception of being a prisoner was to see if you were here to harm us, to gather information from you. I got medical training from a former guest here, a doctor who stayed with us over a year then died of malaria."

"Why were the doctors murdered when obviously they were doctors? Couldn't their talents have been put to good use?"

"They weren't all killed. We were fighting a war against a rival militia, weeks went by. One of the doctors was one of the enemy, he pulled a gun, a fight ensued and three of the doctors were killed. We killed the gunman but not before he did this. They are buried."

"Where are the others Niah?"

"I will not divulge that, they are safe." There was a pause then, "Niah the prisoner is who I would like to be, she represents the good in people. I was taken from my home when I was twelve from everything I knew, my captors were cruel, a girl in a man's militia, they were my family. Eventually I rose in rank as I was molded into a violent thing, I was good at one thing, following orders. Rape was part of my formative years. It caused me to be abusive when loving someone, my anger surfaces causing me to hurt the one I choose to love. You felt it, I can't seem to stop. At twenty-five I murdered our leader, he was cruel. I shared command of the militia with my lover. At thirty he was murdered then I alone was leader, five years now. We now number a hundred and forty, fifty are women though none as brutal as I. This scar on my face is evidence of what was done to me, other scars aren't visible. Torture is rampant in our way of life, you learn to accept it and give it . . . stay with me Max, love me willingly." This was more of a command as she stood behind him now, tall at 5'10" looking formidable in sunglasses and uniform with her hand on her machete.

Max is taking all this in. "We live in different worlds Niah, you, how you survived I cannot imagine. I love my wife and I have a son I adore, my heart is taken whatever you do to me, allow me to return to them."

She removed the weapon from its sheath and held the blade to his throat, she didn't take rejection well.

"Make if quick if you're going to kill me." Max expected the worst.

"Stand up," she told him and took him back to the camp. He was tied to the same tree to rest. Giles and Warren weren't allowed near him as they worked attending to patients.

"He looks better Giles," Warren said, "and he knows who she really is."

"We should end this," Giles remarked. "She's attracted to his innocence."

"He knows the code, he can end it at anytime as well."

Evening came, the prisoners were fed. Niah sat by Max as he was eating.

"Would you ever give this up?" he asked her.

"And live a normal life? No, I am exactly where I want to be."

One of the aides approached her suddenly. "Commander, there is a man here to see you, he has the cargo."

"See to his needs," she told the aide.

Max wondered who had come and what cargo had he brought.

"The Russian," her top general introduced him as such.

"I am the Bolivian Commander," she said as she introduced herself.

"A sense of humor," he said, "I am Remmy."

"What do you have for me?"

"Weapons, the best made, transmitters, everything we agreed on."

"Where are your men besides the transport crew?"

"Two hundred yards away west."

"Stay the evening, tomorrow you'll be paid after testing the cargo."

"Certainly Commander."

Special Ops had monitored this but had no way of alerting Max, Giles or Warren.

Later, Niah came again to Max.

"I heard trucks, large trucks transporting your cargo," he said.

She didn't answer, she sat by him, her head resting against his shoulder, she wouldn't allow him to be alone and segregated. They slept.

Morning came, the camp was active. Niah had gone. The Russian demonstrated the weapons, he was about to be paid when he demanded more. Niah wouldn't budge, there was an argument as more of his men appeared. Then a war started, her troops fired on the transport, they were trying for a takeover.

Max shouted the word, "Extraction, I say again extraction."

Soon the Special Ops commandos moved into the village. Max, Giles and Warren were freed. Gunfire from every direction left wounded. They quickly set up a triage. Children were taken to the barracks for protection. Max looks around and sees Niah wounded. He goes to her, she is conscious.

"You leave and a war starts," he said smiling at her.

She tried to smile, now trying to get a good breath.

"I'm here for you Niah, you will live."

He prepares to operate, she reaches up and touches his face. "Walk from that tree where you were chained, east, through the jungle, three hundred feet . . . the man you seek is there with others, four others underground marked by a black stone—they performed surgery on our wounded, very brave."

Max told the others where to find the doctors then performed surgery on Niah for a collapsed lung, broken ribs and a severe chemical burn. Several from her militia were wounded, only three died. The Russian and his men weren't as lucky, several died. Special Ops had saved the day, five wounded.

"I believe we owe you a thanks my friend," Warren said to Colonel Blake.

"After what we heard and observed you guys deserve a medal for bravery," he turned to Max as he said this, "and abuse."

"She was tormented," Max said, "that was all she knew." He was still operating on her.

"If she lives, she'll be tried for murder and likely spend her remaining years in a Bolivian prison doing hard labor," Colonel Blake told him.

In a couple of hours Max and Giles had finished operating. They conveyed their thanks and prepared to leave.

Warren said, "I've never experienced so much turmoil in one place that seemed so peaceful caused by a woman, Niah touched all of us."

"That is really . . ." Mr. Giles couldn't finish, everytime he thought of what Niah did to all of them he became angry, especially what was done to Max. "Sheriff you have one warped sense of humor."

Warren laughed.

Giles met with Dr. Bolivar who had been freed and mentioned how Dr. Macfarland valued their friendship. "I am his step-brother Giles Fairlane, you've met Max his son."

Dr. Bolivar hugged Giles, shook hands with Warren and Max. "I am most grateful to be rescued, when we return home we'll have a visit and discuss your brother and what he meant to my wife and myself."

All the doctors were rescued, their value having been worth more than gold to the militias. Warren, Max and Giles prepared to leave for home and begin to live normal lives again. All three were glad for the outcome though Warren warned them of these events causing post traumatic stress.

"I've been through trauma, sometimes the effects take time to diminish. Max, you would understand after what Klauss put you through."

"How did you deal with it Sheriff?" Giles asked.

"My advice, make love to your wives, stay busy, therapy if necessary."

"Appreciate all you've done Sheriff," Giles said, "and as you need us on cases we'll help."

They arrived home several hours later. Max and Giles followed Warren's advice. Giles seemed to fall more deeply in love with Marilyn, she felt the same. Their marriage had ended any doubts that he was able to love her completely.

Silvia and Max could barely be separated, she was adamant to give Max a daughter. He left out some details about the trip including the night visitor who tormented him.

Warren darkened the door of a church where he talked to a friend, the residing preacher, face to face about certain aspects of his life. Veronica was upmost in his mind, if he should marry her and subject her to his world of dealing with the negative side of the human race or quit the job he was good at to protect her.

While the three were in Bolivia, the Camp became a town, Hector was elected as Mayor, a police presence from the Sheriff's Department could now be there 24-7. The buildings were nearing completion. The town of Camp Veracruz also had a small church started there. Hector was congratulated by Warren, Max and Giles, the girls joined them in the celebration at a restaurant. They discussed what becoming a town would mean and possibilities.

"So how was the trip to Bolivia, the rescue? Don't leave anything out," Hector said.

"Sheriff, you want to sum it up?" Giles asked.

"Leave out any details you feel aren't pertinent . . . some potentially embarrassing," Max said.

Everyone looked at Max.

Warren looked over at Giles and Max then, "We rescued a friend Dr. Bolivar and any surviving doctors, there was a small war. Giles' army of Special Ops are credited with stopping the war with few casualties and the rescue. End of story."

Everyone expected more details. Hector glanced at his date Nicole. "When I get these three alone, I'll get the detailed version."

Marilyn laughed, soon everyone was laughing. "You should write a book."

"Being factious?" Giles asked her.

"Veronica, has the Sheriff told you anything?"

"Next to nothing Hector."

"When are you two . . . ?"

She looked at Warren then back at Hector.

"Our secret," Warren said. "Veronica has made top realtor in Houston, I'm proud of you," he told her.

Everyone clapped and made a toast. Then they focused on Silvia.

"How is school?" Nicole asked her.

"It's going really well, the teachers are really top notch, I have a tutor who really pushes me, even reading to me in bed, asking me test questions." She was excited.

"That's going over and beyond," Nicole replied with a smile.

The evening was a celebration between friends to honor Hector. The four couples intended to stay close and in contact.

The next week Warren and Veronica went to see a friend Louie Lamour Zimmerman perform in "Memories and Songs of Liberace" produced by Giles Fairlane. He gave Warren and Veronica passes for the best seats. They met with him before the performance. The theatre was large, full of ambiance.

"This is Louie, a consummate performer." He introduces him to Veronica.

"Nice to meet you Louie."

"Likewise." He kissed her hand. "Good to see you Sheriff."

"Thanks for the invite and the tickets."

"How is everyone, those that made it out?"

"Max and Silvia as you know made it out, married, have a kid, living with his uncle Giles Fairlane, who bears an uncanny resemblance to Dante Stephens; he married Marilyn Macfarland. The others I haven't been in contact with. The ghost, I couldn't tell you anything on that one. Dante Stephens was never found."

"Someone should have written a book about this."

"Maybe someone will, not me however, too many loose ends."

"I'd like to take you both to dinner afterward . . . I do have a favor to ask."

Warren countered, "We'll take you to dinner and then ask your favor."

"See you then," Louie said.

Two hours later they were at Roscoe's an upscale restaurant. Louie was excited.

"The performance was remarkable," Veronica told him.

"It was Louie," Warren said, "now what can I do for you?"

"My close friend was murdered, it seems the case was buried, the investigation was abruptly stopped."

"Who was your friend?"

"Milo Jones, also an actor, murdered six months ago. He was a gay activist. I'm asking if you would investigate."

"What do you think happened?" Warren asked.

"We, Milo and I, were leaving a club when a young man began to insult us. He had friends, we left quickly, running. They pursued us for about three blocks then broke off the chase still yelling slurs at us. The next morning I called Milo, no answer. When I arrived at his apartment his door was unlocked, I went in and found him dead. He had been beaten beyond recognition and there were signs of torture. I called the police. At the police station I looked at mug shots, it was dark the night we were chased but at the station I saw the young man, the ringleader again talking to an older man. The older man was the captain, the young man, I found out, was his son. I started asking questions. I was told I was mistaken but the investigation continued for several months then was suddenly dropped."

Warren listened. "I could have the case reopened if we had new evidence Louie or put you in harm's way to lure out the suspect."

"Luke is his name."

"Captain Bill Moseley's son," Warren said.

"You know him?"

"Unfortunately yes. Don't try anything until we have a plan . . . understood?"

"Understood."

"I'll call you."

Louie left feeling that Sheriff Warren would give it his best. Veronica listened intently to all of this.

"Warren, be careful."

"Always am."

"Keep this between us, his life depends on it."

"I promise." They kissed.

He took her home, an hour later he left, stopping by his office. He read files about several attacks on the gay community. One of the deaths was that of a policeman posing as a gay prostitute to draw out the perpetrators who had been killing or maiming gays. Camera footage was solicited from a gay bar where Louie and Milo were last seen together. Warren studied some old evidence and Louie's statement before leaving for the evening.

The next day he requested files from the police who had been on the case. Captain Mosley of the police, the suspect's father paid a visit to Warren.

"Sheriff, good to see you."

"Likewise Bill."

"I heard you wanted to reopen a case, an unsolved case."

"We might just have ourselves a witness, perhaps new evidence."

"I'm anxious to hear," the Captain appeared uneasy, "and certainly anything regarding the case will be shared with your department and vice versa."

"I appreciate your help."

"What is this new evidence?"

"I can't divulge that yet."

"Keep me in the loop."

"Will do."

Warren called Louie, "I'm giving you twenty-four hour protection until further notice. Don't mention any of this even to your closest friends."

"Understood."

Warren got a team together to study the evidence, three employees, one of which was Lieutenant Dawson who had helped him at the Camp.

"A man was murdered six months ago, he was a gay activist . . . don't let this prejudice you, taint the case, just approach it for what it is, an unsolved murder and perhaps a cover-up. This case might be linked to the death of an undercover cop posing as a gay. Say nothing about this case outside the four of us. Milo Jones and his friend Louie were leaving a club late at night when a group of six young men cornered them, insulting and pursuing with the intent of harming them. The next morning Louie found his friend murdered, beaten beyond recognition, signs of torture. Get any information from the club, who was on duty, camera footage, talk to his neighbors . . . we don't have a murder weapon. He might not have had a fair and thorough autopsy."

"We could have the body exhumed if forensics could re-examine," Lieutenant Dawson said.

"A possibility. A theory is that someone may have covered up evidence."

"Let's hope not," Dawson said.

"Everyone, let's get on it, Dawson stay a moment."

"Is it Moseley, the police captain?"

"My best guess is yes, Louie recognized his son as one of the gay bashers. If he covered his son's actions, he's looking at prison time. The chaplain always hears confessions, the captain is a good Catholic. Find out, talk to him, set up a surveillance on father and son. The gay bars will still be targets. We might have an undercover operation and surveillance set up at one or more locations. Louie is going to help us if needed, using his talent for acting."

Veronica was concerned for Warren. "I can't tell you what he's working on but he's burning the candle at both ends," she told Silvia and Marilyn.

Later the Sheriff ordered an exhumation. Captain Moseley tried to stop it as unnecessary. Louie was the witness in this murder investigation, the exhumation was done.

Max, Mr. Giles and the Sheriff's medical examiner re-examined the body thoroughly and found new evidence. Captain Moseley wasn't informed of the new evidence. He decided to do surveillance on the Sheriff and Veronica, Warren expected this.

Months later. Niah escapes from the Bolivian prison and heads for the jungle to her militia and then to America to find Max. She has done surveillance on both Giles, Max and their families learning about them, what they liked to do for activities, saw their wives and Max and Silvia's child.

One evening Giles and Max were working late in a research area of the Free Clinic. They are the last ones to leave. Max is deep into his work as he studies the effect of an experiment using stem cells in regenerative research.

"Mr. Giles? You aren't going to believe this." Max was writing down the results as he looked through a microscope.

"He can't hear you Max," a woman's voice said. Even in the dim light he knew it was Niah. She walked toward him wearing a black dress and heels. "Shocked?" she turned up the lights.

Max saw her, she was beautiful. "Shocked doesn't even begin to describe what I'm feeling now," he was feeling ill at ease.

"What do you think?"

"You look beautiful . . . I'm glad you survived," Max was sincere. "How did you escape?"

"I have friends who made it happen. You kept quite a secret with that army you brought, but in the end they fought the Russians who deceived us."

"Are you still commander of your militia?"

"Yes."

There was a pause, "Where is Mr. Giles?"

"He is sleeping unharmed."

"And the reason for your visit?"

"Direct and to the point . . . to find the answer to one question." She pulls out a pistol, points it at Max, "Someplace private."

He stands up, puts his work aside and leads her to a small office with a bed.

"We are here, now what?"

She stabs Max with a syringe, he falls on the bed unable to fight off the effects of the shot.

"You will answer my question, truth serum mixed with popano," she says. She makes love to him.

"Do you love me Max?"

He resists telling her.

"Do you love me?" she asked again.

He answers, "Yes, I love you Niah."

She wanted more from him but she got the answer she came for.

"When I love someone, I can't express my love except in tormenting them, then I found you but then I began to torment you. I'm giving you your freedom, forcibly bringing you back to Bolivia to be with me wouldn't win your heart. I love you enough to leave you in peace to live your life. Be happy, love your wife and son." She kissed him, he was aware. "I will be checking on you time-to-time." She then left with her aide.

Max heard Mr. Giles calling to him, he struggled to sit up.

"Are you all right Max?"

He got up, dressed and staggered down the hall as he looked for Mr. Giles.

"Niah?" Giles asked.

"Yes, everything is all right. She wanted the answer to one question, if I loved her."

"What was your answer?"

"With an injection of truth serum my answer was truthfully 'yes'."

This revelation startled Mr. Giles. "Is she gone?"

"Back to her militia. I'm not mentioning this to Silvia."

"Nor will I. The results of the stem cell experiment?"

"I had to stop recording the results."

"Tomorrow Max, let's go home."

"This evening has been extremely strange, seeing Niah, in a dress."

They left.

At dinner Mr. Giles and Max were unusually quiet, the girls knew something was up, neither divulged the events of the evening. Both Max and Mr. Giles then went several rounds on the racquetball court.

"Now I know something happened," Marilyn said to Silvia.

Each tried to make Giles and Max talk to no avail.

Silvia was now seven months pregnant but it was rough this time. She had progressed in spite of this in her nursing courses with Max's encouragement and help.

Max and Rupert were continuing a kickboxing regiment helping to strengthen Max's legs and relieve the trauma of the mission to Bolivia.

Marilyn had monumental duties at the museum. One day a man approached her, he wanted information about a particular painting recently added to the museum, a Rembrandt and wanting a private tour.

He was strikingly handsome around fifty. "I met you at an art exhibit a few months ago."

"I do remember you," she said, "Markus Berber, I'm Marilyn Fairlane, you gave this museum a very expensive painting. Let's take tour."

"I was glad to give the painting to such a museum as this, you take great pride in managing it."

"Thank you, but I have a lot of help. And there is your Rembrandt."

He approved of where his painting was displayed. "I am more than satisfied that the painting is appreciated. Do you have time for a cup of coffee?"

They went for coffee.

"Are you married? Engaged? I didn't see your ring."

"You certainly don't waste time."

"Unfortunately I don't have time to waste, I'm on God's timetable and time is running out."

"Why?"

"I have cancer."

"I'm so sorry."

"Don't be, I have had a good run, although a short one. What do you want in life?" he asked her.

"That the man I'm married to will love me as much as I love him."

"I would like to have met someone like you to settle down with."

"You don't know what a pain I can be . . . on good authority I know that an oncologist my husband knows is going outside the box to find cures."

"I've given up, seven years is enough."

"You must explore every avenue and don't give up. Let me connect you with Giles."

"He's British?"

"Very. He's a doctor and a scientist and is informed on the latest clinical trials."

Giles talked with him on the internet and had a face to face conference.

"Researchers at Johns Hopkins are in the midst of a trial using a combination of epigenetic and other therapies to treat people whose cancer has advanced. The oncologist Dr. Isidro is in on these trials, I believe he can help you."

"I appreciate all you and Marilyn are doing for a stranger."

They had him to the mansion for dinner. Giles praised him for the addition of the Rembrandt to the museum. He showed Markus some of his collection of paintings. Markus realized that he was an art connoisseur who had gotten his collection over years of travel and had studied art. He then met Max and the family.

"I never had time for a family. I was always traveling and now . . ."

Giles then shifted the train of thought to a conference with Dr. Isidro over the internet. Markus asked his questions as Giles sat by him and Dr. Isidro explained the clinical trials and the risks involved. He was encouraging.

"It's now my decision isn't it?"

"It is."

The evening went on then as he was leaving he thanked everyone for the special dinner and new friendships, he kissed Marilyn's hand.

"Goodnight everyone," he left.

"He does seem taken with you," Giles said.

Marilyn laughed, "I told him I was married to a very smart, handsome man who makes me feel special."

Giles kissed her. "Let's go upstairs and make both of us feel special."

"Well there they go," Max said to Silvia.

"I need a shower," Silvia said, "join me?"

They went upstairs.

The next day there was a delivery.

"A dog? Giles? There is a note. ["Gone to see Dr. Isidro, would you mind taking care of her? She is family, will contact you over the internet on my progress—Markus"]."

"I don't see a problem, we should keep her," Giles said.

Everyone seemed excited at having the small brown and white Sheltie named Allison. Max and Little Giles were especially taken with her.

Back in Bolivia shortly after Niah's return, she talked privately with one of her high ranking officers.

"I have a mission for you Captain Ruiz. I'm sending you to America to give me reports on one of the prisoners, a doctor, Max Fogel and his family. Advise me how he is doing, if he is happy and his health is good. This is a mission that is important only to me."

"I accept and will comply Commander. How long a duration?"

"Not sure, you are somehow to infiltrate, probably through their Free Clinic where Max and his Uncle Giles, also a doctor, take in patients who cannot pay."

"I remember both of them."

"Protect them as you can, as necessary."

"When?"

"Leave as soon as possible."

Niah would communicate with Captain Ruiz by coded message over the internet or cell phone.

Rita entered the Free Clinic as an immigrant who was living on the street. A nurse brought her to Max and Giles. She spoke in Spanish. Max immediately asked the nurse to get the information from the woman.

"Apparently Mr. Giles, she has no living relatives, has been living on the street for years, is a legal resident from Mexico. We could begin examining her now, she has no place to live, however there is a community center blocks away."

"What is she needing?"

"I really haven't determined that, she isn't forthcoming about certain ailments. She generally has soreness in her pelvic area, hands and feet."

"Then start from head to toe," Giles told him.

Max attempted to give her a pelvic exam, she refused pointing now in the direction of Mr. Giles. Mr. Giles did the exam. She then allowed Max to continue the overall physical.

"I think she likes you," Max said.

Giles smiled, "She's messed up under the hood."

"How bad?"

"Bad . . . cysts, evidence of abuse, a pregnancy."

"I noticed cuts on the arms, neck and legs also evidence of a stabbing with severe consequences," Max said.

"Don't treat her any differently, careful in pressing for answers."

"Agreed, obviously her time on the streets was tumultuous."

"We should take her to the Community Center."

"Or home?"

Giles thought for a moment. "We could allow her to stay here at the Clinic for the duration of the tests. Home might come into play if she were an employee."

"We could always use the help." Max and Giles knew better. "We could pretend we needed the help."

"Then it's settled, I'll make arrangements for her to stay here through tomorrow."

They told her, she was grateful.

"I need a job," she said.

"We'll see what we can do," Giles told her, "first things first."

They left her there in the care of a nurse.

Giles and Max became recently involved in a project concerning the epigenome's role in directing genes to behave in certain ways. Markus Berber was a test subject involving a combination of epigenetic and other therapies to treat people whose cancer had advanced. The researchers would investigate the epigenetic markers to predict and treat various conditions that have challenged the medical community. Dr. Isidro brought Mr. Giles and Max into this research recently upon meeting Markus. They were also researching stem cell tissue regeneration which was funded by grant money. Both were very busy. Marilyn knew how their involvement might save Markus.

Silva and Marilyn were glad to meet Rita Ruiz, she was very quiet at first. They took her to the beauty shop, to lunch sometimes as possible. She now worked at the mansion and seemed genuinely grateful for the doctoring she had received including major surgery at the Free Clinic. She was appreciated and respected by the family. Max and Giles came home tired but always included her in one of the meals to socialize. She gradually opened up. She would contact Niah once a week, no one else was aware of this. Mrs. Bradley didn't totally trust her but pretended to. Weeks passed.

Events at the mansion began happening quickly. Silvia suddenly started hemorrhaging and was rushed to the hospital eight months pregnant. She was given drugs to stabilize her and to keep the child. There was no explanation, then very soon, she fell into a coma, her breathing stopped. Max, Mr. Giles and other specialists were there trying to save her not knowing why this happened. Days went by, Rita was at the mansion with the staff taking care of Little Giles. She had called Niah earlier and brought the child to the hospital to comfort Max and check on Silvia.

Max held the child as he sat by Silvia, "We're going on two weeks now. I remember when our situations were reversed and you spoke to me. I heard some of it like I was dreaming. If you don't come back to me, they will be burying two of us." Rita heard him talking, it touched her heart. He then talked with Mr. Giles.

"What haven't we done? What have we overlooked?"

CHAPTER XVII

A Flower for Silvia

Giles was standing beside his office desk at the hospital, Max sat, he was keeping it inside as best he could as he held the child.

"Mary had three miscarriages and died in childbirth, the child as you know didn't survive either. I did years of research only to come up with no definitive answer."

"Mr. Giles, if Silvia dies I won't survive it." Mr. Giles listened as painful as it was to hear. "I'm asking you and Marilyn to consider raising Little Giles if . . ."

Mr. Giles kissed Max on the head as he hugged him. "It might not come to that, don't give up yet Max." He then held the child.

Rita called Niah that evening. "Commander, Silvia is dying and her unborn child. No one, not Max or Mr. Giles nor other specialists are able to save her. She has been in a coma, life signs are weak."

"And Max?"

"Devastated."

"Let me talk to him."

"Dr. Fogel, there is a call for you on my phone."

Max was puzzled, he stepped out of the room to take the call.

"I believe I can help Silvia."

"Niah?"

"Just listen—when all the options are gone there is always one more . . . I'm giving you one more."

"How did you know about Silvia?"

"My Captain has been there since I left, Rita Ruiz."

Max glances at her as he listens.

"Here in Bolivia, there is a flower . . ."

Max interrupted, "I don't have time for fantasy or folklore."

She continued, "I don't deal in fantasy . . . this flower is two days journey from our village into the mountain. The flower must be used correctly. I will tell you how to proceed. I ask you one favor when you come, my general is dying of cancer, see what you can do."

Max thought for a moment.

"Do it Max," Rita said, "take this last chance you're being given."

"Agreed Niah, when?"

"Come now, two of my men will meet you at the airstrip and take you in, come alone."

Max talked with Rita.

"My orders were to protect you and your family, to let the Commander know how things were going. I needed your family, I have no one but the militia and I got too close . . . I am being truthful." She became emotional. "If the Commander is willing to help, accept her help, forgive my deception."

"I am almost getting used to being deceived. Take care of them, don't tell anyone until you have to." Max hugged her.

Several hours later he arrived by private jet, he brought gear to scale the mountain along with two changes of clothes and boots. He was met by two soldiers on horseback. They arrived at the village six hours later, it was late afternoon.

"Niah."

"Max."

"My captain?"

"She is home looking after the family," he didn't comment further.

"We leave at daybreak," she said.

"I want to examine the General."

"It's bad," she said.

"What treatment has been given?"

A doctor comes to the tent where the General is and introduces himself. "I'm not an oncologist, but I have been giving him treatments with these medications which I have listed for you."

"The cancer is then in his liver and hasn't matesticized?"

"As best I can determine, only there."

"I'll be in contact with an oncologist in America by internet so he can advise us."

Max took a break and called Mr. Giles.

"An explanation Max," Giles said frustrated that Max didn't tell him.

"My apologies Mr. Giles, only one of us could come. I am here at the village in search of a cure for Silvia. There is a type of flower growing on the side of the mountain where we will be in two days, it is said to have healing properties. A wild goose chase, I don't know. The Commander, two soldiers and myself will leave at dawn tomorrow to retrieve one and take it to the airstrip to be sent to you with instructions on its use. The Commander's general is now my patient, I will need Dr. Isidro to instruct us over the internet . . . I will appreciate your efforts Mr. Giles on Silvia's behalf."

"Be careful Max, contact me and I'll let you know if there is any change. Dr. Isidro will be in contact. Good luck."

"Take care Mr. Giles."

"Are you hungry?" Niah asked him, she heard the conversation.

"Not really, sleep is all I need."

He removed his boots and prepares for bed. She puts on her night ware. He turns to see her, how muscular and slender she is.

"If I run into trouble, you can protect me," he said.

She walks over to her cot next to his, she kisses him on the cheek then goes to sleep. He expects her to come onto him but she doesn't. Confused by her behavior he falls asleep quickly.

The next morning Max checked the General then they left for the mountains.

"How do you know about this flower?" he asked her.

They were going as fast as they could on horseback navigating through the dense jungle.

"Later," she said.

His thoughts were of Silvia and Little Giles. He would give this his all, successful or not.

Several hours passed, evening had come, they made camp for the night. They ate.

"The flower?" Max asked.

"The flower is no fantasy. When I was fifteen, I almost died from an assault on our village by a neighboring militia. I was given the job of a lookout, several of us did this as part of our training. I was beaten severely as the enemy moved in. Someone found me and brought me to this mountain. The man who found me was dressed differently as were the inhabitants, they weren't carrying guns. He talked with the others there then brought a white flower, removed it from a pot and placed it across my chest along with the soil. I couldn't see the others but heard them conversing in a language I didn't understand. Then I don't remember, everything went dark. When I woke up I saw the man who rescued me. The flower was wilted and removed. He smiled. I asked him why the flower? He understood me, he didn't speak my language but he communicated. I was to tell no one about the flower. He brought me back to the village, I asked him to stay, he did. I never knew why but as time went by I realized that this man from that village was one of the guardians of that mountain where those flowers grew. He then became my protector, it was his choice, he never returned as he adopted our way of life . . . we called him the General, now dying from cancer."

Max was intrigued by this.

"The flower is only used to help the innocent, it wouldn't work on him now and not again on me. We will try to bypass the guardians and get Silvia that flower, these people don't carry guns but I assure you they are capable of killing to protect what they consider sacred. We must sleep now to get an early start."

Max thought over the information Niah had given him finally sleeping.

The next day they traveled hours before reaching the base of the mountain. Leaving the horses behind they walked a half mile. Max prepared the rigging, Niah insisted on going first. The climb was very steep, the rocks were unstable as Max held the rope from below as she climbed to forty-five feet. Niah reached for a rock to place her foot to steady herself.

"We have to have the flower and roots intact," she told him. "I almost have it."

"Careful Niah."

"If I could reach farther . . . got . . ." She cried out as she fell.

Max helped break her fall holding onto the ropes from below but she twisted her ankle. He checked her. "Where are you hurt?"

"My pride and my ankle."

"You have a severe sprain," he determined by a quick examination. He carried her some distance away from the mountain.

"Be careful," she said. "Where are my aides?"

He listened but returned to the climb. It was a long reach but at eighty feet he got a flower and with a knife dug up the roots with soil. Carefully cradling it he made his descent.

"Niah, I've got the flower. Niah? Where are you?"

He walked back into the jungle, suddenly he was met by three men in strange clothing, looking more like the guardians Niah had described. One took the flower from him, a man about forty with short cropped hair. He was then taken to where Niah was being held inside a small circular structure. The man motioned for Max to sit, he did. He sat across from him on the dirt floor, the flower between them. He talked but Max didn't understand. Then he touched Max on the chest across his heart. He spoke again and Max understood. He knew Max was hurting, the stolen flower was for healing someone he loved. Now probing deep into Max's past, the man looked into his eyes and saw into his soul.

"I sense your pain where your wife and unborn child are concerned."

Max then pulled out a picture of Silvia and their son, the man took it and after studying it laid it by the flower. He concluded that Max had no ulterior motive for taking the flower other than to save those he loved, he had an innocence about him. Max was now instructed as to how the flower, roots and the soil were to be used. The flower was given fresh soil and handed to him in a metal bowl.

"Thank you," he told the man, a tear rolled down his cheek.

"You are going back to heal one of us known as the General, he lost his way when he left to protect one brought back with a flower." The man then looked over at Niah. She didn't understand his words, his language was spoken and understood only by those he chose.

"Will I be successful?" Max asked him.

"In healing your wife or the General? I cannot say, you must hurry now."

They stood up, Niah's aides were allowed to leave with her and Max. Max was feeling an urgency to save both Silvia and the General but his spirit seemed less burdened since talking with the Guardian.

Two days later Max called Mr. Giles. "A messenger has taken the flower to the airstrip, there is a jet waiting with orders to take the flower to you, its use is very specific. Call me when you get it . . . if Silvia . . . I'm staying behind in the village to help Niah's general with his cancer. I'll be in contact with Dr. Isidro."

"I'll be here, try to be, as you say positive, we mustn't give up now."

"Until then," was all Max could say.

Then the waiting began.

Max and the oncologist corresponded listing drugs and treatment given to the patient, the General. He would guide Max and the other doctor in determining precise treatment and biopsy analysis for that particular cancer. Two other doctors now introduced themselves, recent recruits from another militia wanting to learn from Max and the oncologist as they assisted.

The General staged a gruff, obstinate side as Max hooked up his I.V. and physically checked him. "You have been with the others?" he asked referring to the Guardians.

"Yes sir, I have, they said you are one of them so I must save your life whether you want me to or not."

"Then I better behave myself." He was grateful for the care he was receiving even as he showed his rough demeanor.

There were other wounded that were attended to as well.

Night came, he asked Niah if the doctors were prisoners.

"They were recruited," she replied, "doctors here are as valuable as gold."

Max didn't pursue it further, he contacted Mr. Giles who had given him up dates on Silvia everyday for three days.

"Silvia is improving, not out of the woods yet."

"Would you turn the camera so I can see her?"

He does. "Three days improving."

Max had a guarded optimism concerning her condition, he feared another failure.

"What about the child?"

"Still hanging in there . . . you look tired Max."

"Thank you Mr. Giles for pointing that out," he laughed.

"It's good to hear you laugh. When are you coming home?"

"My patient, the General needs me. I made a promise to help him and there are three other doctors here, I can add to their training before I leave. Somehow they are getting the necessary medicines for the cancer treatments. I don't know how or where."

"Take care of yourself Max."

"And you Mr. Giles, the Commander sends her regards."

"Until tomorrow."

Niah then walks in, "That was kind of you."

"You heard? Silvia is improving and is still carrying the child."

"And my general is improving, I'm glad Max."

"Why a flower? Your suggestion saved two lives."

"I heard three lives."

Max knew what she meant.

She dressed for bed resisting the urge to make love to him, she laid down on her cot by his and they slept.

Five more days passed. Max had gotten the news that Silvia had improved significantly. The flower and roots had rotted and were removed along with the soil off her chest. He prepared to leave.

"I want updates on the General's condition, he has responded well to the treatments, still grumpy."

Niah smiled.

"Is my captain allowed to stay? She has become very attached to your family."

"We've gotten attached to her, she's welcome to stay."

He walked over to Niah, put down his luggage and kissed her.

"Behave yourself," he said.

As he turned to leave he felt a firm pat to his rear end. He stopped for a moment then saying nothing else he left. Niah watched him, she knew they would see each other again.

He had called Mr. Giles, the jet was waiting. He was anxious to see Silvia and also had concerns about Niah and the General. Several hours later he arrived. Mr. Giles met him at the airport.

"Welcome back." They hugged.

"Good to be back."

When they arrived Max greeted Marilyn and headed straight for Silvia who had been moved home a week earlier. She was sleeping.

"She is still on an I.V., has lost some weight, but her life signs are good and breathing on her own . . . no explanation Max, we have ideas as to what caused this but nothing definite, the flower is equally a mystery."

"I appreciate all you did. I'll be here with her tonight . . . and Little Giles?"

"Here he is right now," Rita brought the child.

Max held him. "And you Rita practically putting me on the jet to get me there, thanks isn't enough." He hugs the child lovingly, "Now to bed with you." Rita puts him to bed.

Max kisses Silvia and lies on the bed beside her. Mr. Giles leaves, an exhausted Max then falls asleep.

The next morning Silvia awakens.

"Max?" She says in a weak voice.

He stirs.

"Max."

Now awake he kisses her. "Pretty girl you had all of us worried."

"I don't know what happened?"

"Neither do we, just theories. See that flower, its roots and soil are why you're alive. I travelled to Bolivia to bring you one, we'll discuss that later."

"The baby?"

"The baby seems fine, the pregnancy will probably go full term. Mr. Giles and I had you taken to the hospital then you were moved back here a week ago."

Silvia's energy was depleting.

"Go to sleep, we'll talk later." He held her hand until she fell asleep. "My patient, the General, is improving thanks to Dr. Isidro," he told Mr. Giles. "I told Niah and his doctor to contact me with updates on his condition."

"From what you told me about him and his people I have more respect for the effort to save his life, not for him."

"These people are unknown to the outside world simply called Guardians. Had we tried to clone the flower, it would have died without helping Silvia protecting its secret."

"Hector was notified, he came to the hospital as often as he could. I explained where you were, he saw the flower after she was moved home, he knew you would do anything to save her. The Diaz's came and stayed off and on."

"I'll call them." Max said.

The next morning Mr. Giles found Max sitting beside her asleep, he awakened him.

"I was reluctant to awaken you but there is an update concerning your patient, the General."

"Thanks Mr. Giles." He checked Silvia first.

"Max, her readings are almost normal."

"I . . . ," Max couldn't finish, he was filled with so much emotion, he kissed her then contacted the Bolivian doctor treating the General.

Giles was listening, "A good report?"

"So far the treatment is working."

"And Niah? Only if you want to talk about it."

"When she decides to visit me, she is suddenly here with her aides and then there is nothing I can do but cooperate wherever and whenever." Max was angry over her ability to dominate. "I did nothing to bring this on."

"I know that Max."

"She confused me this last trip and made no advances."

"Probably to catch you off guard."

"I am restrained by her for the duration. I told her I loved her with truth serum administered, only the one time. If I were interested in her and I assure you, I am not and attempted to hold her and initiate making love, it triggers her tormented mind to harm the one doing the act. She could harm any of us or as she had told me once, considered taking me forcibly back to Bolivia. I owe her for saving Silvia. With luck she'll tire of me and find someone to love her without maiming them. Silvia is all I need and want, I love her unconditionally."

Silvia was still asleep as Max and Mr. Giles continued to talk. A nurse then stayed with her as Max and Mr. Giles left to continue research downstairs in the lab.

The next morning Max was eating cereal in the smaller kitchen talking to Mrs. Bradley, sharing his cereal with Allison the sheltie. Suddenly Silvia and the nurse walked in.

"I'm fixing breakfast, anything."

She kissed him, "Anything?"

"Your favorite?"

"Yes," she said as she studied his face tired and stressed. "You went through a lot to get me well."

"I couldn't let you go."

They continued to talk as he fixed breakfast.

"I love you Max and whatever the problem we'll face it together."

He turned to look at her. "How is number two?" he asked as he touched her stomach trying to be comical.

"I know it's a girl and she is fine."

"What problem?"

"If there is a problem, you seen stressed, preoccupied."

"Silvia, I almost lost you and number two as well. I have been stressed since this whole incident began, traveling to Bolivia to find a cure in a flower or just a hoax."

"Who told you about the flower?"

"Why the questions?"

She stopped questioning him, they ate together he began to relax.

Two months later. Niah returns with plans to take Max and follows him to his office with two of her aides. She tasers him, he passes out and falls to the floor. Silvia and Rita arrived to meet him there. Rita knew what she was planning when she saw Max, she disagreed with Niah's plan.

"You'll be killing him to separate them."

"I'll fill him so full of drugs he'll cooperate and do anything I ask with no thought of her. Have you grown soft Captain?" Just then she saw Silvia.

"Wiser maybe. I'm still a formidable warrior, not on your side it seems."

Then Silvia who wasn't allowed near Max, walks toward her, "Please don't take him Niah."

"I saved your life and that of your child."

"And I'm grateful. Will you tire of him and leave him maimed or worse? Filling him with drugs? I want my husband."

Niah comes toward Silvia and Rita as do her two aides. She produces a knife. Silvia and Rita begin to defend themselves. Silvia is pushed hard against a wall by one of the aides, she screams in pain and falls to the floor.

"The baby . . . the baby is coming Rita."

As Niah and her aides move in on the women suddenly three men appear and stop the assault.

Six months had passed. A war has started with another militia. Niah is fighting with her troops defending the village, the triage is treating several wounded. Max is there operating and giving the orders as senior doctor. There is also a cholera outbreak which started before the war began. Hand grenades had done the most damage. The rival militia wanted to capture the doctors to treat cases of cholera as well as the wounded. Max began suturing a wounded man's arm who had also contracted the disease. Niah was now inspecting everything in the camp, the wounded and damage done.

"I can't believe they were able to descend on us so suddenly, our sentinels will be interrogated," she told Max. Five wounded, two dead, otherwise they left empty handed. The medicines are safe for now." Niah kissed him, "I need you now."

"Allow me to finish suturing the man's arm, he might like to keep it."

"All right, five minutes."

He told another doctor, "Have him moved with the other cholera patients."

He then entered her tent, removed his boots and clothes.

"I dreamed about my wife and children last night."

"You miss them?"

"Still do, no matter, you'll make me forget them in time."

"I have a shot for you," she said.

Unknown to her was that Max had analyzed the drug she had been giving him and with an antidote had given himself shots to counteract its effects.

"It hasn't erased them from my mind totally, not yet."

After she gives him the shot she gives one to herself.

"I want to love you now, hold me Max."

"And lose which body part? A hand perhaps . . . you want your men restrained."

"All right, I'll love you."

"You have a strange, distorted way of loving someone Niah, you kill them in some manner."

She continued to love him, he had developed a numbness to her touch but it was still unpleasant.

Days went by, the General was now civil to Max, the doctor who essentially got his treatments for cancer on track. He wasn't allowed to contact anyone he knew, it was devastating to him. Niah had punished the sentinels in some manner, some lost privileges, some a finger, others were reduced in rank for allowing the enemy militia to attack so easily.

Several of the prisoners from the attacking militia became sick, there were children taken to be used as slaves who were vulnerable to the cholera as the epidemic worsened.

"Niah, let me vaccinate the children being held," Max suggested.

"Absolutely not, we need those vaccinations, they'll grow up as our enemies."

"Five, only five."

"No, end of discussion."

She saw the frustration in his face as he turned to leave. She punished those who didn't follow orders.

Over several hours, as he watched the prisoners dying, he couldn't stand by doing nothing. He took five vials of vaccine and immunized each child but not the adults. He explained that there wasn't enough for everyone. He left quickly hoping he wasn't seen. Another doctor saw this but said nothing.

That evening Niah talked with him.

"Those who don't follow orders are punished Max."

He looked at her, "Who told you?"

"No one had to, there were five vials missing, five children. One of the children will die."

"No, do to me what you will."

"Oh I will, come with me." She had one boy released then killed him in front of Max.

He was trying to hold it together as he was forced to watch. She then brought him to the tent. He was devastated to tears.

"The boy could have been retrained," he said.

She didn't punish him further.

Max decided to take matters in his own hands. Six months had seemed like an eternity. He punchered himself with a contaminated needle used on a patient suffering from cholera. In so doing he became sick very quickly. He was then moved to a barracks.

"Why did you do this Max?" Niah asked him.

"Since I was never vaccinated for this before being kidnapped it seemed the only way to leave here, this time you won't win."

Niah sat by him, tears flowed, "I wanted you to be with me."

"But you didn't consider the repercussions, you've killed me already taking me from my family and everyone I knew. I have done the only thing I could do, die . . . and the images of you killing that child."

Niah and two soldiers leave as others tend to him. She goes to the mountain for help from the Guardians. One appears, she begs for help humbling herself.

"It is too late," she was told.

When she arrives back at the village Max is dead. Two of the other doctors are there but couldn't revive him. She was devastated. A Guardian appears to her suddenly, now she is back Max's office.

"Am I in torment?" she asks. "Was that reality?"

"That wasn't reality, this was to demonstrate to you what you would have done, what he would have done, he is alive as you can see. This is part of your torment."

One of the men checks Max, as he comes to, he recognizes the one who had communicated with him earlier concerning a cure for Silvia. Another assists Rita in delivering Silvia's baby. The third keeps Niah and her aides from harming anyone and from leaving. She becomes frightened, unusual for her, as she remembers part of the torment she just experienced. The child is a girl as Silvia predicted.

"These men are Guardians in the jungle," Max told Silvia, "protectors of that rare flower I was allowed to give to you."

He stood up as one of the Guardians speaks.

"We have come to stop this chain of events. This child must survive, you and your wife must survive. As a family you will teach her values and love as you are teaching your son. We must leave and take the Commander and her aides."

"What will happen to her?" Max asked as he knelt by Silvia holding the child, having no knowledge of a future that never happened.

"Are you asking for leniency?" one of the Guardians asked.

"Mercy," he said as he looked at Niah.

"She will be trapped in her jungle never to harm you, your family or anyone."

"For how long?" Max asked.

"As long as it takes, the punishment imposed on anyone saved by a flower who harms another is harsh. She will learn this way. We are very aware of events all over the world even with an unborn child, occasionally we have to intervene especially when one was innocent and saved by a flower which is sacred to us."

"Will the flower make her special?" Silvia asked.

"In some ways yes. We must go." They were also going to take Rita.

"Allow her to stay," Max said, "she defended Silvia."

"It is done," the man said.

Max turned back from Silvia and saw Rita but not the aides or Niah. He called for those in the clinic where his office was to take Silvia to the hospital wing, then he called Mr. Giles. They named their daughter Flora.

Niah often thought of Max as she was forced to relive all the unhappiness and pain she had caused so many and was glad that Max hadn't died.

Max and Mr. Giles were involved in research, still on a new project, the Free Clinic was overflowing with new patients, they seemed to thrive on helping people. Racquetball and chess were two favorites they shared. The girls had tennis. Silvia continued her nursing courses while Rita helped take care of Flora and Little Giles. Marilyn was busy with her museum duties as assistant curator. Veronica and Warren would visit as they could, her real estate business had grown, she kept busy. Rupert and Max continued kickboxing. Rupert was called in on some research projects.

Max would watch the usual graphic programs about surgery on cable with Mr. Giles and Little Giles in his arms. He and Silvia had given him a play doctor set and also a little weight to lift as he is watching kickboxing.

Mr. Giles is amused. "Let him watch cartoons occasionally Max, he's still a child."

"I will, I want to round out his education."

"Max, he might have nightmares," Silva said.

"About kickboxing or surgery?" he asked humorously. "Come on Little Giles, let's go lift weights, Mommie doesn't want you to have nightmares."

They did then he put the child down for a nap. Silvia had already put Flora to bed.

She watched Max continue his regiment of lifting weights. "That's still a turn on," she said.

"You're still a turn on," he told her. "I like to watch your pretty legs when you play tennis."

"You have anything on the books today?" she asked.

"That research project with Mr. Giles."

"I have a two hour course on computer then can you tutor me?"

"Yes, but I reserve the right to keep you after school for some reason, I'll think of one."

They make love.

"I think about the Guardians time-to-time, if they hadn't intervened twice I wouldn't have you," Max told her.

"Well I'm not going anywhere unless you end up in the jungle again. I also think about how she was going to take you and their intervention to stop her . . . do you think they're still watching us?"

"Maybe. She is now within her jungle probably living in torment as she relives every moment."

"Maybe she will change."

"That would be something. I hope she does."

CHAPTER XVIII

Mistaken Identity

Giles and Max discuss a conference that will take place in London in a month on regenerative research as it regards the use of stem cells.

"Could you and Silvia accompany Marilyn and me? Would her schedule allow any missed classes? This would be Marilyn's and my honeymoon—business vacation."

"Certainly I'll talk with her, how many days?"

"Six, three for the conference, three to sightsee."

Silvia was as excited as Max when he told her. She and Marilyn had a very close friendship and both knew how similar Max and Giles were in their behavior, especially about research, attending several conferences, meeting with other scientists.

"I'm going," Silvia said. "Max can tutor me to make up for the missed classes."

She and Max agreed. Little Giles and Flora would stay with Silvia's parents.

The month of the conference came, they landed at Heathrow Airport in London. Marilyn as assistant curator of the Metropolitan Houston Museum wanted to tour two museums in London, one was dedicated to paintings, the other to sculpture.

Meanwhile at Scotland Yard, "We have confirmed through biometrics that Dante Stephens arrived at Heathrow Airport eight hours ago. Do we arrest him now?"

"No, have him followed."

"For him to return here and put himself into our hands doesn't make sense."

"It doesn't unless he's brokering an arms deal or planning a heist."

Everyone was tired as they arrived at the hotel. They ordered in. Mr. Giles was anxious to see London again.

"I brought Max here several years ago to a conference."

"I was impressed even then," Max said, "he lectured students here on behalf of research."

Marilyn and Silvia were listening but were planning their own agendas. They all succumbed to the need for sleep.

The next day Giles and Max attended the first session at Oxford University where Giles graduated, a forty minute drive from London. The scientists got acquainted.

"Dr. Fairlane, Dr. Fogel welcome, I'm Dr. Rhodes. Dr. Macfarland was well respected, we were sorry to hear he died. We have invited only those who have worked with stem cells, so let's get started."

There were fifty in attendance.

The girls had a small sightseeing tour in the city, shopped, caught up with Giles and Max.

"How was your day?" Marilyn asked them.

"The conference was energizing. Max and I were with other scientists some of which I had met before, I had to pretend otherwise as Giles Fairlane."

"How were you two while we were occupied?" Max asked.

Silvia laughed, "We had a fun day, took a small tour and shopped."

"Let's eat," Marilyn said, "Giles?"

"Sounds good."

They ate at a small restaurant discussing the conference and the tour the girls took through London seeing Saint Paul's Cathedral.

"I'm jealous," Max said.

"Let's go to the Museum of Art tomorrow if you fellows are up to it after the conference," Marilyn suggested.

"Deal," Giles agreed.

Someone had been following them since their arrival in London undetected.

Giles and Marilyn made the most of their honeymoon. She had become accustomed to the new Giles, his blonde hair and goatee. He would wear vests and small circular glasses as he did before the transformation.

"Certain things you do really turn me on," she said.

He smiled, "As what?"

"What you're doing now."

They made love.

The next day at the conference someone came over to Giles during a break, Max saw her.

"Dante, where have you been?" she asked.

He was so startled that he didn't know how to reply.

"Say something, I've been aware you were here when Chief Constable Williams had you followed once you entered the country."

"You have me confused with someone else."

Max then walked over.

"Call me," she gave him her number, "it's important." She was blonde, forties, slender and very persistent.

"What was that about?"

"I have no idea but apparently Dante Stephens was into some covert activities and that woman knew him. Don't mention this to the girls."

"I won't Mr. Giles."

"The conference is starting again."

Three hours passed.

Max called Silvia, "We're on our way."

That evening they decided to see a musical instead of going to the museum, they had been given tickets by Dr. Rhodes. Afterward they ate at a well known restaurant that Giles and Max had been to some years earlier when visiting England attending a conference.

That next day the conference began.

"We enjoyed the musical Dr. Rhodes."

"I'm so glad. Unfortunately our guest speaker is ill, would you and Max consider being substitutes answering questions about your research on stem cell tissue regeneration?"

"Max?" Giles asked.

"It's ok with me."

"And if you would mention the research done by Giles your brother."

"All right," Giles said.

They got to it, it was a very busy day as both Giles and Max answered questions for over an hour, then others discussed their own research. As the conference ended for the day, the girls were called, dinner first and then to the Courtauld Gallery. The museum was one of the premier museums in the world housing priceless art works and sculpture. Marilyn was in her element there as was Giles who had amassed a fortune in art over the years.

He had wandered away from the others as he looked at the art. A voice from behind startled him.

"You didn't call."

"Who are you and why are you following me?"

"Daniella. Why are you speaking with a British accent and pretending you don't know me . . . who gave you that scar on your neck?"

Giles was perplexed. "How did I know you?"

"I'm tired of this charade."

"Please indulge me, how did I know you?"

"Our involvement in covert activities and there were the other activities."

"Whose side in the covert category?"

"That depends . . . you're masquerading as a scientist now? I'll be in touch, try to get your memory back," she said with sarcasm and left.

The others caught up with him. He talked with Max about the woman and what she said.

"Scotland Yard was mentioned, that I'm being followed, not just by her. I'm obviously a wanted man."

"Should we leave, go home?" Max asked him.

"I'm not sure we'd be allowed to leave the country. If we're stuck, let's go have fun," he said.

"Ok," Max agreed.

They all spent most of the evening hitting the night spots around London, finally so tired they were about to drop they returned to the hotel. Both rooms had been ransacked.

"Conference," Max said to Mr. Giles, "tell them."

Giles began, "This is happening because of mistaken identity. Dante Stephens was into covert things, Scotland Yard believes I am Dante, biometrics surely confirmed this upon our arrival in England. A woman claiming that we had worked together has been following me, I'm not sure what I'm going to do about it."

"Giles, I think you should go to Scotland Yard and talk to the Chief Constable who has obviously been searching for you," Marilyn suggested. "This woman might even be working for the Constable."

"A possibility," Giles said. "First though we have three days left, perhaps more if I can't leave England . . . let's go do something else."

"Possibly the woman will contact you again."

"I'm not sure I want her to."

They ended the day continuing to clean the mess the thieves had left.

The next day they embarked on a tour of Windsor Castle and the National Portrait Gallery, housing some of the most famous portraits ever painted. They stopped briefly for lunch. The manager came over to Giles.

"There is a call for you."

He took the call.

"I must speak with you, there are two assassins on your trail, you double crossed them."

"I did no such thing," he replied. "It's the woman," he told them.

"Meet with me," she said.

"Where?"

"Outside, across the street."

"All right."

"Was that wise?" Max asked him.

"I don't know." Max followed him outside but stood in front of the restaurant.

"Who is that?" she asked.

"My nephew, more like a son to me, we do research together, my wife is in the restaurant."

"Married? Who knew you'd marry one of them. I would be surprised if you don't have a communicable disease." This kind of talk wasn't pleasant to hear.

"What about assassins coming after me? What about our rooms being ransacked?"

"I don't know about that last one unless they found you."

"Why, how did I double-cross anyone?"

"If you can't remember then there's no reason to talk to you about this and possibly avoiding a painful death."

"I will say it again," Giles was frustrated, "I am not who you say I am. If I am wanted, why a trip to a science conference in England where assassins are waiting for me as well as the police and a woman I can't remember who is incredibly beautiful."

"Memory loss for real?" she said.

"Well apparently. Who do you work for?"

"The Chief Constable who might be willing to help you, he helped me. We worked, you and I with the two who are after you, art heists, arms deals. The Constable's close friend was working undercover on this last heist, he was killed by one of us, it wasn't me. You took the money and left England, left me, that was two years ago. I was proven innocent of the death and began to turn my life around working with the Constable. I spent six months in jail, a much lighter sentence in exchange for my help."

"I can't apologize for something I didn't do, I am sympathetic to the incidents that transpired especially where the Constable's friend was concerned and what happened to you. What can I do?"

"Come with me to Scotland Yard, look at the wanted pictures, see if that could trigger some memory. I know you said you didn't do these things but seeing the wanted posters might make you aware of those who are after you."

"I'm going to talk with my nephew and my wife . . . coming?"

"I'll wait here."

As Giles left her he heard a scream, she was being abducted. Max quickly approached Mr. Giles who called Scotland Yard, Constable Williams.

"I need to have you here Mr. Fairlane or whatever you call yourself now."

Giles arrives with Max, Silvia and Marilyn. The Constable won't shake his hand as he introduces himself, he notices the scar on Giles' neck.

"Somehow you were involved in the murder of one of my policemen during an undercover sting."

"I was not."

"Do you have a twin? You can drop the British accent."

"I don't have a twin, now about the young woman known as Daniella."

"Did you get a good look at the van? You said it was a van?"

"Yes and so did my nephew."

"Black, Mercedes van, delivery type, black tires, no wheel covers, license plates missing, two men, white, one with long brown hair, six feet and the other white with a gray beard, short gray hair about six-two, both wore green coveralls." Both Giles and Max agreed on these facts . . . "Oh, and the one with long hair had a prominent scar on his left cheek."

The Constable was impressed with the details they gave.

"Dante . . ." he said.

"Giles Fairlane," he countered.

"Take a look at these pictures and I'll show you the two men pursuing you. Daniella had identified them several months earlier. If they make contact, try to stall them and get as much information from them as you can until we come up with a plan. I'm going to use your help."

"I'll do what I can, our hotel was ransacked last evening, they know where to find us."

"I'm sending an undercover operative to protect your family, go home, I'll contact you. We must figure out what they plan to heist, what you stole from them, rescue Daniella and tie up all the loose ends."

"I didn't steal from anybody, I didn't murder your friend, how can I prove it?"

He didn't answer Giles. "Here is my operative, Lieutenant Wayne, take them home, their rooms at the hotel we assume were broken into by the two that kidnapped Daniella. We'll be in touch, rest if you can."

Once back at the hotel they weren't allowed to go out.

"We can order in if you like," the Lieutenant told them.

They did. They had finished cleaning up the mess left by the intruders then occupied themselves reading or playing chess.

"Lieutenant, do you play?" Giles asked.

"Yes, as a matter of fact."

Giles and Max were playing quickly. Silvia and Marilyn stopped their card game to watch.

"Check," Giles said. Then as Max studied the move and countered, Giles declared, "Checkmate . . . it happens." Giles grinned.

"I'll get you next time," Max told him.

"Lieutenant, join me please."

He did. "It's been a while."

The game began, the Lieutenant knew chess very well. He began to ask Giles about himself trying to find out what he knew while engaging in the game. Giles managed to answer questions while concentrating on the game.

Finally, "Checkmate", declared the Lieutenant.

"Good game," Giles told him, "anything else you want to ask me?"

"I was purposely distracting you and you let me win. Yes I would like to ask you, do you have any knowledge of who killed our operative?"

Giles and the Lieutenant looked eye-to-eye, "No sir, I don't."

"I'm a good judge of character and it seems to me you are either a pathological liar or telling the truth, I am leaning toward the truth."

Everyone was listening.

"He is telling the truth," Marilyn said.

Max and Silvia didn't comment, they went to their adjoining room for the night. The Lieutenant stayed with Giles and Marilyn.

"It will be safer this way."

Giles agreed, "That sofa looks pretty good."

"It will be fine, just call me Wayne, no formalities."

Everyone settled down for the night. Wayne went to the small kitchen sat down and began cleaning his firearm, checking every part of it. Giles walked in, he sat and watched.

"Recognize it?" Wayne asked him.

"No, I'm afraid I don't know much about guns. As a boy in Dorchester I went dove hunting with my father, we used rifles. I was never inclined that way in the use of guns to his disappointment."

Wayne told him, "This is a Glock 26 pistol, Dante Stephens had one just like it, he also knew a great deal about making bombs, seemed to come naturally to him."

"My son, I mean my nephew Max and I are doctors, we are also in the field of science, no bombs."

"Daniella was following you as you and your nephew answered questions about stem cell research at a conference at Oxford. She said it didn't sound rehearsed."

"Because it wasn't."

"Tell me Mr. Fairlane what's going on?"

"Giles will do. Test me, lie detector, anything."

"Anything? Truth serum?"

"If the questions don't go too far, we, like all families, have our secrets."

"Your accent isn't fake, very authentic. Dante never became close to anyone as you are with your wife and nephew. We'll start with my testimony then a lie detector test then who knows. How did you get that scar?"

"Your testimony?"

"I've already found out a lot about you Giles, I'm very observant. The scar?"

"Someone tried to murder me, I can't talk about it now."

"I won't bother you further tonight, I'm turning in."

Giles left him.

Marilyn knew they had been talking, "Are you all right Giles?"

"I'm all right."

They slept.

In the night there was a call on Giles' cell phone, Wayne had setup a recording device for Giles' phone and the hotel phone.

"They are holding me Dante, they want you and the money."

Wayne was signaling Giles as to what he should say.

"How do I get you back Daniella? What money do I owe them?"

Someone else then spoke to Giles, "You double-crossed us Dante, it's going to cost you, think on that one." He hung up.

Everyone including Wayne was nervous. Max and Silvia were listening then closed their door again.

The next day they all had breakfast in the hotel. Wayne called Constable Williams about his observations and the late night call. Voice analyzing equipment would be used both for the caller and Giles. Everyone was brought to Scotland Yard. The recording was then analyzed. Giles' voice pattern didn't totally match that of Dante Stephens, the voice of the kidnapper was analyzed but there was nothing in the voice database to compare it to.

"There are some odd things about all of this," the Constable told them, "Daniella had taped conversation from her two partners, excluding Dante and this voice recorded last evening matches nothing we have, so there is a third person involved that Daniella is now aware of." The Constable then begins to ask Giles more questions. "Where were you on the night of August 22, 2010 when my operative was killed?"

"You'd never believe me," Giles said.

"Try me."

"Couldn't you just give me a lie detector test?"

"Yes, and we want to question your wife as well?"

"Who are you Mr. Fairlane?"

"A scientist, a doctor and a husband."

"You were still in London when the murder occurred, witnesses. Bring those forward to attest to your whereabouts on August 22."

"What about Daniella?"

"I am certain we will hear the kidnapper's demands. Can you imagine what they'll do to you? To her?"

An hour later Giles got the call, Wayne had retrofitted his phone to record anywhere, they were in an unmarked police car headed to the hotel.

"This is what we want, then we call it even. Assist us on a last heist. Meet us at the Mark Museum at Londonderry and Bay in one hour."

"What about Daniella?"

"We'll talk about that when you get here, no one else."

"Understood."

Wayne called Chief Constable Williams. "They want to meet with him sir in one hour, the Mark Museum."

"I'll at least know what they look like and their names," Giles said.

"Just make sure you don't tell them you're going by another name."

"They'll ask why I came back to England."

"You could say to make another heist involving art, a painting perhaps."

"Max?"

"I don't think you should do this, it might be a trap. Where is help if you need it?"

"A valid concern," Wayne said. "It's up to you but since Dante Stephens ripped them off I don't believe they will harm you, at least not until they get their money. Daniella might have been compromised. I hope she hasn't changed sides, she does hold a grudge against you."

"What do you think Marilyn?"

"I don't know Giles, it's too dangerous, I don't want to lose you again, but if they aren't caught you take the fall for the crimes."

Wayne had observed them very carefully and didn't comment.

"All right," Giles said, "what now?"

"Let's stop here, you will arrive by cab. What do you know about art?" he asked as he called Scotland Yard to send an agent in a cab for Mr. Giles. "I can bring in an art expert to help you in this."

Giles smiled, Max laughed. "I don't need anyone else," Giles told him.

"What's so humorous?"

"He has spent several years analyzing art," Max told him.

"Giles spotted two fakes at the Metropolitan Houston Museum where I work," Marilyn said.

"How did you come by this talent?" Wayne asked.

"I love art, always have. I'm not an artist myself but I worked with others as an art conservator for a few months at the John Paul Getty Museum in Los Angeles."

Wayne was impressed.

The cab arrived, Agent Scott would wait for Giles at the museum, pretending to take a break, he would listen recording the meeting.

"What have you done to yourself?" one asked him, "glasses, goatee, that scar on your neck?"

"Someone tried to murder me."

"Too bad they didn't succeed," another told him.

"You must be Holt."

"You know darn well who I am."

"I'm Shay, you left me for dead."

"So where is Daniella?"

"Checking out a painting . . . you're going to help us steal it."

"You believe I stole from you?"

Shay punched him.

"Which one of you killed the agent?"

Daniella walked into the room before there was an answer.

"Dante, your face is bruised."

"My name . . ."

She stopped him before using the name Giles.

"Have it your way."

"You aren't really needing to be rescued are you?"

"No and I duped you into coming here."

She and the two others escorted Giles into the gallery of the museum. There was a previously unknown Van Gough on the wall. There was security and a crowd. They weren't suspicious of these four. Daniella hung onto Giles' arm, the other two dressed in suits split up. The gallery was huge.

"That Van Gough is worth several million," Daniella told him.

"I recognize it from the news but nothing like seeing it in person."

Giles got closer. "It's a very good fake," he told her after a few minutes examining it.

"What are you saying?"

"Obviously I know a thing or two about art . . . that is a fake."

"Keep your voice down, what makes you so certain?"

"The brush strokes, it's almost a perfect fake but look here."

They got as close to the painting as possible as he showed her small details which proved it wasn't an authentic Van Gough.

"When was it most likely painted?"

"Probably by a contemporary or more recent, I can't be sure without studying it closely."

"The curator here might be interested to know this," she said.

"He probably does."

"This is the one to steal," she said.

"It's a fake."

"Trust me."

"Are you working both sides?"

"Yes, I appreciate the fact that you wanted to rescue me. Let's go."

They met the others outside.

"We'll tell you when and where," Holt told him not knowing it was a fake.

Giles was there alone when he saw the cab again.

"They are planning to steal a fake."

"That was a test for you and yes that is the one that will be stolen. I was able to record most of the conversation. Looks like you were punched."

"By the unpleasant Mr. Shay, what do you mean a test?"

He drives Giles to the hotel to meet up with Wayne and the family.

"No one could know all that you do about art without years of study."

"Good day Mr. Fairlane," the agent says as he leaves him at the hotel.

Giles is exhausted.

"Daniella," he told Wayne, "seems to be playing both sides but expressed her loyalty to the Chief Constable."

"You now realize that the fake will be stolen?"

"Yes."

"You have apparently studied art extensively."

"I have. Can we go out?"

"As in out there? Too dangerous," Wayne told him.

They ordered in a favorite, pizza. Wayne enjoyed himself. Silvia called home, Max listened in.

"The kids are fine," Rita told her. "Your parents brought them home today."

"Everything is fine here, no problems, we'll be a few days longer."

Rita didn't believe there were no problems.

"Have a good time," Rita told her, "how's Max?"

"I'm behaving myself," he told her. "Take care."

"You think she believed the part about no problems or you behaving yourself?"

"I believed you," he said, "she knows I rarely behave myself."

They turned on the music and danced until they were exhausted.

"At least Max got lucky," Giles said to Marilyn. Then he looked at Wayne who wasn't about to give them any privacy. Marilyn was about to laugh.

"We have to talk about strategy, Giles."

"I'm all yours," he said.

Wayne was concerned for his safety. They discussed several strategies and scenarios. Giles struggled to stay alert but succumbed to exhaustion and sleep. Marilyn, still awake covered Giles with a quilt as he slept in a lounge chair, removed his shoes then said goodnight to Wayne as she went to bed.

Giles wasn't to steal the art but going back to the museum with Daniella and with the blessing of Scotland Yard pointed out three more likely fakes. Two undercover operatives, a security detail were nearby dressed as patrons of the museum.

"What are your feelings about this?" she asked him.

"The curator is probably in on it. If he switched the fakes for the real he's making a great deal of money without Shay and Holt. Having them steal this fake Van Gough and he might actually know it's fake, is to have them take the fall for any crimes already committed and the blame away from himself as he continues to make money switching forgeries for real. If your loyalties aren't with Scotland Yard then I'm a dead man for telling you this."

"Let's go," she said.

They met with Shay and Holt.

"We're ready," she said, "Dante tells me this recently discovered Van Gough is worth millions."

"When?" Giles asked them about the heist.

"Tomorrow evening, the alarms will be disabled," Shay told him.

"Do you know how many alarms are in this place?" Giles asked Holt.

"Several, we've got it covered . . . let's go."

"Where are you going?" Shay asked Giles.

"To be with my family."

"No, you stay with us until this is over."

Giles then said, "At least allow me to call them."

Daniella nodded yes.

"I'm going to be late, something has come up, I'll be there tomorrow."

Marilyn was worried. Wayne who stayed with them passed on the message to Constable Williams.

Daniella and Giles went to a hotel joining Holt and Shay, they then discussed things apart from the others.

"I still want to know why you left me . . . I went to prison."

Giles looked at her, "I'm not the man you knew. If I explained it, that there are no memories, would you believe me?"

She sat by him on a sofa and cried, he held her. Daniella did believe him but it still hurt. She wanted him but since he wasn't Dante Stephens she didn't force herself or him to get to know each other again. They were in one of the two bedrooms.

"I can take the couch," he said. "Daniella, will I ever see my family again?"

"I hope so. If Winston is in on this, we may all die."

Holt and Shay talked business with a collaborator by phone.

The next day came, plans were finalized. There was to be a Patron of the Arts Party at six P.M. at the museum.

"I have no suit with me," Giles said when he was made aware.

Daniella and he went to a nearby shop, he bought a suit, she bought an evening dress then back to the hotel, they were given passes to the party by Holt.

Giles commented to Daniella, "These invitations come from higher up, someone in on this heist."

Holt and Shay would be dressed as maintenance personnel. Two agents from the police were there posing as attendants for the soiree. It began. The curator as well as his assistant came and talked to the guests. There was music, food and wine. Giles fit in perfectly as an art connoisseur.

Daniella cautioned him, "If you know too much especially to the curator it could blow the heist and they'll know you aren't Dante."

Giles heeded her warning.

They again looked at the Van Gough. Daniella brushed by one of the agents who quickly put a wide bracelet on her as she took off a similar one handing it to the agent all unseen.

"What was that about?" Giles asked.

She didn't answer. "You look very handsome."

He smiled, "And you are beautiful."

The evening went on finally ending several hours later, they went back to the hotel.

Shay and Holt later disconnected the wall alarm. Winston, the curator shut down the power as Holt and Shay took the Van Gough. They were channeled out an office entrance, T.V. cameras, alarms, all security systems went down. Security came soon after. Winston pretended to be drunk and said there wasn't a problem, he had cut the power accidentally which he now restored. He thanked them and went home.

After the art is stolen Giles becomes a prisoner of Shay and Holt. Daniella is with them. They drive several miles to a warehouse. They tie Giles to a chair and open a small case containing truth serum.

"Why are you doing this? You said everything was even if I helped you."

Just then Winston, the museum curator, walked in. "Has he told you anything?"

"He will." Holt administered the serum.

"Who murdered the agent?" Giles asked before he succumbed to the drug.

As Winston looked at Giles he said, "You're looking at him."

Daniella had thought Dante had killed him, now she knew the murderer.

"Where is my money?" Holt asked.

Daniella had on a bracelet tracking device and had hoped the police had followed.

"I don't have your money. I'm not who you think I am."

"And who are you?" Winston asked.

"Giles . . . Macfarland . . . you switched other works of art like the Van Gough you wanted stolen . . . I can spot fakes, did you tell them?"

"He doesn't know what he's talking about."

"I detected four fakes."

Holt was outraged. "Is this true? You took the profits, you had us steal a fake. Why?"

"So both of you would go to jail for all the previous heists," Daniella said.

The anger he felt caused him to be irrational. Taking his focus off Giles he pulled a knife on Winston. Shay joined in. Daniella ran out the door to give the police a stronger signal from her tracking device which she left outside and ran back inside to help Giles. Winston shot Holt who had stabbed him. Shay assisted Holt. The police were closing in.

"Where is your bracelet Daniella?" Shay asked. "You had it on, when you came back it was gone."

Shay is about to shoot her, the police arrive.

"Put down your weapon, only one chance to live," Wayne said.

Shay reluctantly surrenders. Max enters behind the police. Giles is still under the influence of the drug but he is freed still sitting in a chair.

"I'd like to ask him some questions," the Chief Constable said to Max. Everyone else stepped outside with the exception of Wayne, Daniella and Max.

"What are you going to ask him?"

"Something I must . . . Giles, state your full name for me."

"Giles Macfarland."

"Are you a doctor, scientist and an art collector and conservator?"

"Yes."

"Did you murder my agent? Answer truthfully."

Daniella then said, "Winston, the museum curator confessed."

Giles answered, "No, I didn't murder him."

"Why do you look like Dante Stephens?"

There was a pause, "He murdered me, then . . ."

"I can finish for him," Max said. "Mr. Giles is my father, Dante Stephens murdered him, then Dante was murdered. Dante's mind was purged of any and all thought and memories while on life support and my father's mind was transferred in. I had my father who was 85 back in the body of a 41 year old. The scar was from whoever murdered Dante, we haven't determined who did. Working quickly we saved the body as well as the brain patterns and memories of my father . . . end of story."

Constable Williams just sat for a few moments trying to digest what he had just heard as he looked at Giles.

"Has this been done before for anyone?"

"Never successfully. I don't know how much time he has but we have him back, his wife has him back, he's the same person."

Giles was coming out of it. "I look in the mirror everyday at the face of my murderer and this scar reminds me that Dante had enemies."

Max continued, "How this affects things for justice we don't know."

"Pretending to be Max's uncle, I call myself Dr. Giles Fairlane since Giles Macfarland was murdered and doesn't now exist to anyone."

"This is the ultimate drug to find the truth. With the testimony of Lieutenant Wayne, Daniella, your son, observing you and your family I have formed an opinion. It would be wrong to allow you freedom if you were Dante Stephens but even worse to deprive you of living, how be it a strange existence looking in a mirror not recognizing yourself ever."

"Seeing my murderer every day, reminding me of what he did."

"Can this experiment be duplicated?"

"No one can tell, the conditions were apparently in sync or it wouldn't have worked," Max told him.

"I regret your loss Constable," Giles said.

"Winston will receive the maximum punishment, anything you have told us here won't be revealed to anyone else. I'd like to visit you and your family in America at a convenient time."

"That makes two of us," Lieutenant Wayne said.

"It would be a pleasure to have you and Wayne come. I miss England at times, perhaps my wife and son will visit with me."

"Perhaps. If there are others who are after Dante Stephens then there could be problems ahead for you. In the meantime the crime of murder will be deleted from the most wanted information on Interpol and Holmes, our database." This satisfied the Constable, he and Giles shook hands. Daniella kissed Giles on the cheek and said her goodbye. The two thieves, Holt and Shay would go on trial for various robberies, Winston would have the added charge of first degree murder. This ended the pursuit of Dante Stephens in England.

CHAPTER XIX

Free Clinic Woes

"You don't look poor." "Why don't you get a job?" "Being a veteran doesn't give you a free ride." "Why did you have children you can't support?" "Free medical help isn't a right."

These words and phrases appeared at one time or another in the Homeless Weekly News published by Rupert Schmitt. These cruel remarks were said by some in society about the poor even appearing in articles in the Daily News. He was Max Fogel's good friend and schoolmate for several years. He emigrated from Germany about the time Max did and did scientific research with both Max and Mr. Giles time-to-time which caused him to be well off financially. He was also a doctor who practiced at their Free Clinic two days a week. He had made it his mission to expose crimes against the poor on the street. His weekly newspaper was published by willing help in a small building in downtown Houston and reached 10,000. He went to various shelters with an assistant offering medical help and also to those on the street, encouraging those needing more serious medical attention to be treated in a hospital environment.

Kickboxing brought back memories. Rupert made it a weekly habit to spar with Max and as often as possible to enjoy an evening meal with him and his family. He was envious of how Max's family had completed him.

Mr. Giles had fun telling on Max and Rupert some of the funny happenings while they were in school. Rupert was amazed everytime he was around Mr. Giles at his transformation.

At this most recent gathering, Rupert talked privately with Max after dinner.

"There is something I must tell you."

"Sounds serious."

"It is. When we were two wild boys in school I slept with a girl, I wasn't wearing protection that night. I think I got her pregnant, she never said but two months later she dropped out of graduate school. I would have done the right thing . . . she moved a week later. I never heard from her again. You were the smart one and took precautions."

"Not that many girls, I was envious of you, always they liked you."

"Don't kid yourself, you had a following."

"You never found her?"

"No, but I think I have a son living on the street. I saw him a week ago at the shelter where he was fed then he slept on the street."

"This is startling, what did he look like?"

"Like her and like me, now about twenty years old, his name is Matthew Grey."

"How did he look?"

"Had some whiskers, dark brown medium length hair, blue eyes, about six feet like me. He was wearing a silver band on his right ring finger had a cross on it. I gave a ring like that to his mother Sarah."

"Have you spoken to him?"

"Yes, I introduced myself as a doctor and if he had any medical needs I would be glad to help him. Then I asked him if he had relatives. A mother who was in a mental institution and didn't remember him—he had no one else."

"What are you going to do?"

"That's the question I can't answer."

There was silence for a moment then Max in an attempt to lighten the mood said, "Remember when we used to stage fights showing that we could defend ourselves to the other students? Some actually wanted to fight us."

"Oh yes, you gave me a black eye then I almost broke your nose. We drank German beer, got drunk occasionally and I asked you why you always wore black and suspenders, you never told me why."

"I've almost dropped the suspenders, they still occasionally come in handy. I don't even know why I chose black."

"Maybe rebellion?"

"Mr. Giles came to the school and talked with both of us. He offered to tutor you as well if we didn't get in fights and told me the consequences if I continued the behavior. I really had anger issues when both my parents were killed suddenly, he was my mentor and I respected him and what he did for me, I didn't want to disappoint him."

"I respected him as well."

"Of all the things he suggested, kickboxing to help with the aggression. A form of discipline," he said. "Then things seemed to get better as you and I became sparring partners."

In a while they joined Mr. Giles and the girls. Max showed off Little Giles and Flora. They had a good evening.

Rupert and his assistant Angie continued to treat the street people and gather news from those they encountered. Some of these people were transients, others were permanent residents of the streets. Angie also did census reports for the City and found that some residents were missing. She interviewed two who were pointing fingers at the police, even describing how they were mistreated.

"They said they were looking for drugs," one said, "then pushed and shoved, sometimes the one giving the orders hurt people. When they left, one car with four cops, two came back later in the same car."

"What time?"

"After midnight . . . I could hear the large clock at St. Andrews chiming."

"What happened?"

"The main cop, who gave the orders, beat a man and his partner didn't stop him, they took him away and we haven't seen him since. He would get his pension checks cashed five streets over like several others here . . . he had gotten his money before the police came."

"Did you see their faces?"

The other man, who had been silent, said "I did, in the light of the fire." One of many small fires started in barrels for warmth.

"Would you be willing to identify him?"

"Maybe."

"Do they come here often? Once every few days, once a month?"

"Days," one replied. "There are others who have been taken from other communities like ours."

"Did they ever come back?"

"No."

"Don't tell anyone what you told us . . . ok?"

"Ok."

Rupert didn't give them money so as not to encourage them to lie. "See you soon," he said.

"Bring her back when you come."

Angie smiled.

Max had encouraged Rupert to contact Sheriff Warren.

A day later he called. "Sheriff, I'm Rupert Schmitt a friend of Max and Mr. Giles, we met a while back."

"Yes, I remember you, how are you?"

"That depends. My assistant and I work at the Free Clinic off and on but mainly taking the doctoring to the shelters and individuals on the street. We are getting reports of certain police roughing up the street people in the guise of looking for drugs. Some of these people are missing at different locations, some or all of their pension money is stolen after being cashed, two residents told us, they also told us about a cop, higher up apparently and his partner beating an individual and taking him away never to be heard from. They said the missing man went by the name Friday, that's when he got his veteran's pension money every month from a check cashing store five blocks away."

"That's quite disturbing. I'm working a case where similar disappearances are happening in the gay community, people go missing and later turn up dead. Don't call the police yet. Come to my office."

"When?"

"Come now if it is convenient."

"Be there soon."

Around noon that day they met, a somber reunion.

"This has happened at other communities. I just considered that they were probably transients but not after hearing this. I have a small newspaper published weekly, the homeless are featured as well as their needs, concerns and feedback. Our observations are also noted. The shelters are rated. The Free Clinic is mentioned for possible care." He then gave Warren a copy.

"In the case of the gay community it isn't the police but young people. A friend who is a gay activist identified a cop's son as a suspect in a beating incident after he taunted them threatening harm. It is now a murder investigation. Max and Giles did another autopsy on the murder victim with one of our medical examiners."

"I'm planning to stay in that community on Hall Street, not in the shelter but on the street with the two men who might be able to identify them."

"Be careful Rupert, these cases might be connected. Take these photos with you . . . only one in the four is a suspect the others are plain clothes detectives."

They exchanged cell phone numbers.

"How often do I call?"

"As often as you need. If you call through the department only speak to me and don't leave your real name, as a precaution tell them Mark."

"Thanks Sheriff . . . by the way I think I found my son out there on the street."

"Your son?"

"It's a strange situation, the mother and I dated in school, she and I became estranged later. As best I can figure she became pregnant and moved out of town about two months later. I tried to find her then I found him which makes me fearful for his safety. He's twenty he told me. I have to do something to help him."

"For now the only advice I can give you is to get him to stay inside the shelter for now, show the two witnesses the pictures. Keep in contact."

Rupert then left feeling that he had an advocate to help him.

Warren had a gut feeling that Captain Moseley was involved and that his son Luke had killed Milo Jones, Louie Lamour's friend and perhaps an undercover cop posing as a gay actor.

The next day Rupert called Warren. "One of the two men identified the policeman, Captain Moseley, nothing with the three other pictures."

"Sounds like they were telling the truth," Warren said. "How did it go with your son?"

"I didn't see him last night, I'm worried."

"I'm sending an operative there, Alex Mayfield, he'll fit in as a new tenant and contact you."

"How will I know him?"

"Tall, big, tattoos."

In the meantime Warren and his team had studied the records of Captain Moseley, concerning the murder of Milo Jones, he had reluctantly loaned them to the Sheriff. Then personal records were acquired about the Captain and his son Luke without their knowledge.

Lieutenant Dawson pointed out, "Luke has had anger issues throughout his teenage years and they continued. Arrested on DWI charges, malicious mischief, nearly killed a man in a fight, all swept under the rug by his father and his connections."

Warren read out loud about Captain Moseley, "Anger issues, reported to have said that, 'the streets will one day be given back to the citizens, clean the streets of the homeless, take away their drugs and they'll leave voluntarily.' He has an ally in the Mayor who I suspect cleaned up his son's record."

Meanwhile at the shelter Alex arrived, he was tall, bearded, hair combed back, tattoos, muscular, "a perfect fit," Rupert thought. He offered medical help knowing who he probably was.

"I'm Alex."

"Rupert."

Alex then entered the shelter for a meal as he pretended to be a resident of the street and would report any incidents of brutality on the homeless.

"We're giving vaccines for the H1N1 along with the regular flu vaccine, no charge," Rupert told him.

"Let me think about it."

"Who needs to be vaccinated?" Rupert asked as the shelter became crowded for dinner. A few consented, Angie took information and assisted him. Rupert told everyone he would return in two days. The men who identified Captain Moseley promised to tell no one. No one but Rupert and Angie knew about Alex.

As Rupert and Angie were leaving, Alex asked for a flu shot, "I need one."

Rupert obliged and whispered to Alex, "I'm returning tonight in disguise, I'm trying to find my son."

"The Sheriff told me, I'll be here, hope you find him."

Night came, Rupert was walking up and down the streets looking for his son, he arrived at the shelter and sat a distance from Alex as they waited, nothing was happening. Rupert sat on the sidewalk.

Then about 2:00 a.m. a police car pulled up, two policemen approached those on the street, this time Rupert was frisked.

"No drugs man," he told them as they shoved him seemingly not recognizing him. Alex was trying not to intervene which could blow the investigation or get one or both of them killed. Then they left Rupert and went inside. In the meantime a young man was headed for the shelter, Rupert recognized him and quickly walked in his direction.

"Don't go in, the police are hassling the residents." They then moved around the building and out of sight. "Not all the police are doing this."

"Rupert? You look different."

"I'm trying to observe why the people here are being hassled and are disappearing from the shelters and the streets, I thought you had."

"Not yet."

"Don't give up Matthew, things will work out."

"I've been homeless going on three years, guess I can wait a while longer."

"You might stay the night in the shelter, more protection."

"Too many rules."

"But it's your life."

Just then Angie and Alex caught up with them.

"They're gone for now," Alex said.

Angie then said to the young man, "There might be a job that would keep you off the street." As she said this she looked at Rupert.

"There is our newspaper The Homeless Weekly News, we have a staff . . . if you reported any news to us, took interviews, probably took less in salary than some other jobs, we could use you."

Matthew thought for a moment, "When?"

"Submit for a drug test, no alcohol, leave now."

Matthew hesitated.

"Is that a problem?"

"No, I can pass a drug test and I rarely drink, but why are you doing this for me?"

"Because we want to."

To have been on the street Matthew hadn't grown sour nor bitter, he had given up, he accepted things but he had a great deal of disappointment and frustration to deal with.

"Go with Angie, Alex will be helping me investigate any incidents tonight, my camera will be ready."

"You be careful," he said to Rupert. They left.

"Looks like you put your son out of danger."

"Sometimes the homeless can't see any other life but being homeless. People don't completely trust them or give them opportunities."

"How common is that?"

"Very. Worse if the education isn't there, if drug and alcohol habits persist, much worse; for some reason I trust him not just because he's my son."

Across town, Louie and the Sheriff made plans. Dawson and Warren would pretend to be bartenders in training at a gay hot spot, a bar where Luke and several thugs liked to go gay bashing. Cameras were set up from several angles. Louie would be performing there on a small stage. Signs were made and placed outside announcing his performance 'Song and dance from Cabaret'. Warren and Dawson watched the bartenders and learned. They wore bright shiny silk shirts and black pants as they were dressed by one of the members, both wore wigs.

"We all dress to impress," one man said and laughed.

Louie came over to give his opinion. "A bit underdone but you both will pass."

No one but the manager and Louie knew they were the Sheriff and his lieutenant. Warren checked Louie who was wearing a transmitter. "Looks secure, can you see any problem performing with this attached to you?"

"No problem."

Luke was watching from a car down the street. He seethed at the thought of that gay establishment vocally advertising Louie Lamour's performance that evening up and down the streets and by putting fliers on the cars. Luke called his five cohorts who had participated in cornering Milo Jones as he beat him to death. They now made plans to hurt those who were in that establishment. Luke didn't know that a man he had also murdered was an undercover cop who he thought was gay. He wanted especially to harm Louie.

The music got louder in the bar. Two gay patrons had hit on Dawson, he was embarrassed, one even pinched him when his back was turned. Warren wanted to laugh but restrained himself.

"Show them you ring Dawson," he said.

Dawson did as he said, "I'm taken," then he pointed to Warren and said, "he's not wearing a ring."

The gay patrons turned to Warren who said, "I'll get you for this Dawson." Dawson laughed.

About midnight Louie had finished his two performances. Warren and Dawson had served enough wine, beer and other spirits to get nearly everyone there drunk.

"There's no way around this, we have to try and keep them here," Warren said. He was concerned about possible DUI and DWI incidents. A few people had left. The manager became concerned when six men, all young entered soon after. They carried baseball bats and other lethal paraphernalia.

"What can we do for you boys?" Warren asked them then he saw Luke. The young men then started beating the patrons and trashing the bar. Warren, Dawson and the manager got their baseball bats and went after the men.

"Grab Louie," Luke said.

"Why? So you can kill me like you did Milo?"

"Something like that," Luke whispered.

Warren chased them, Dawson wasn't far behind. The manager checked on the injured patrons. Warren called for backup. He and Dawson followed a distance behind in an unmarked SUV. They could hear Louie begging for his life, he was wearing a transmitter and had also been implanted with a chip tracking device.

"That transmitter has a range of a half mile," he told his deputies who were following in another car some distance away. "We are also recording, no sirens, stay well behind us."

Louie was taken to a remote area, everyone got out of the SUV. Louie and the six men faced each other, the headlights of the car would reveal his execution.

"What are you planning to do?"

"Anything and everything, it's after midnight, no one around, any last words?" Luke asked him.

"Answer one question Luke Moseley."

Luke had a baseball bat in hand as the others moved in. "Do you know who my father is?" He asked Louie as if to intimidate him.

"Why did you murder my friend Milo Jones? He didn't deserve that."

"He was a freak like you. I took great pleasure in delivering the death blow after they finished with him, he suffered."

"There is something else." Louie was trembling from fear.

"What?"

"You murdered an undercover cop, four months ago, red hair, wore black leather, in his forties."

Luke looked at the others then grabbed Louie around the throat. "How did you know he was a cop? We didn't."

"But you murdered him."

Luke didn't answer and didn't deny it.

"Let's get this over with."

He hit Louie and broke his arm, Louie cried out in pain, the others moved in.

"Did you kill the cop?" he asked again.

"Why would it matter? If that guy was a cop, then I killed a cop."

He struck Louie again, he fell, then the sound of gunfire as several shots rang out not striking any of the six purposely.

Warren was there, "This is a warning, put down your weapons, this is the Houston County Sheriff's Department . . . you are surrounded." Warren's deputies had also arrived.

Luke, defiant as always raised his bat to strike a lethal blow to Louie. Another shot was heard, this time killing Luke. The other five were arrested. Louie was taken to a nearby hospital.

Warren told him, "You did good Louie, you'll have justice for your friend."

"Is he dead, the bastard who killed Milo?"

"Glad to say yes and the confession he gave you concerning the murder of an undercover cop. Now we have to deal with his father. Anyone we can call for you?"

"My friend Bill is on his way."

"We'll have someone stay with you just to be on the safe side."

"By the way, what happened to the silk shirts, pants and wigs?"

"We had to look like police again," Dawson said, "get some rest."

Across town Angie has taken Matthew to Rupert's apartment.

"He has food in the frig, help yourself, over there is a sofa."

"You both are unbelievable."

"Why?"

"You don't know me and yet you bring me here, off the street, offer me a job, aren't you afraid I'll steal something?"

"Don't worry, we'll expect a return on our trust in you."

"That's supposed to be a return on our investment."

She smiled.

"Sounds good."

They sat and talked.

"Are you and Rupert . . . ?"

"No, we work together, we have been close friends for years. Rupert has made it his mission to protect the homeless and give them a voice."

"I almost feel like I know him."

"A lot of people say that. He said something about your mother . . . if this is something too personal to talk about I won't ask."

"It's fine. I never knew my father. She is my only living relative, now in a nursing home when I could no longer care for her, her memory has deteriorated."

"I'm so sorry. What do you want to do with your life, your goals, besides not being homeless?"

"Well . . . I was attending college taking accounting but had to drop out as she got worse and the money ran out."

"What facility is she in?"

"Bay City Nursing Home."

"It's . . ."

Just then the phone rang, "How are things?" Rupert asked her.

"Matthew is settling in for the night."

"Would you stay with him Angie till I can get there? It might be morning."

"Sure, I will. How are things there?"

"No more activity yet. No one was taken."

"Be careful," she said.

The next morning Alex told Rupert the news, "Someone was taken from the shelter on Fourth Street, he had cashed his pension check hours earlier."

"Were there any witnesses?"

"No. Strange thing, cashing his pension check was probably known only by the one cashing the check on Lexington. We'll have to test out that theory."

"A sting? I'll do it," Rupert said.

"I will, I'll need the Sheriff's help."

"Then I'm staying, I could document with my camera."

"It's up to you. It could get ugly."

Alex talks to Warren. "I'll need a printed veteran's check, service card, license to match, stats in the computer by this evening." He told Warren the latest news and what he and Rupert discussed about the check cashing and tie to the disappearances. "Rupert wants to stay and document the scam, perhaps more."

"Try to keep yourself and Rupert out of harm's way, assistance will be close. Also, Luke Moseley is dead, the Captain will be aware soon. I can't keep a lid on this for very long."

"Understood, you and Dawson ok?"

"Ok."

Rupert called Angie, "Another was taken after cashing his pension check. Alex is going to be the bait tonight."

Angie was worried but supported his decision to stay and help Alex if needed.

That evening someone approached Alex as he stood outside the shelter handing him a pension check and other requested I.D. and then without saying a word walked on. Alex walked over to Rupert.

"Got my check and I.D. to cash it."

"When will you?"

"In a few hours, let's stay out here."

"You aren't carrying a weapon are you?"

"No, it could cause problems if I'm frisked."

"Then what defense?"

"I was also given a wrist watch, it records, it transmits but doesn't look fancy. The Sheriff's men are here somewhere."

About eleven p.m. Alex makes his move to Lexington Street and acts as if he isn't totally cognitive or coherent. "It's $1500 dollars he told the cashier. How much is your take?"

"Twenty percent."

"That's robbery."

"Take it or leave it."

"Cash it."

"Need your I.D. That's $300 for me, $1200 back to you . . . where did you fight?"

"Iraq, I can't really remember everything about it." Alex staggered away as if he were on a drug. He walked back toward the shelter then a police car came about ten minutes later, followed him then pulled beside him.

"Need a ride?" one asked him. It was Captain Moseley and another policeman.

"I don't," Alex said and walked on. He recognized the Captain but not his partner.

"We think you do, get in."

Alex walked on, the two stopped the car and proceeded to stop him. They frisked him.

"Any drugs?"

"No."

"Well look here, money. Is this from a drug deal?"

"No sir, it's money from my pension check."

"I don't believe you," the Captain said. "We'll keep this while we investigate."

He was then shoved. "You're crooks."

"Careful son, what you say can shorten your life, since you have a distance to walk."

"Since I can identify you?"

"Come with us."

Little did they know that Rupert was using a small movie cam documenting the whole shakedown. Captain Moseley did hear a click and turned toward the sound, he walked toward it.

"Come out," he said.

Rupert quickly removed the film, hid it and walked over to the men.

"You were taking pictures?" He takes the camera, "No film?"

"You're a murderer, your son was a murderer, have you spoken to him lately?"

"What do you know about my son?"

"I heard he died."

Captain Moseley knocked Rupert to the ground, Alex was now held at gunpoint regretting that Rupert had told the Captain about his son.

"Are you the doctor who comes to the shelters?"

"Yes."

"Why did you say my son is dead?"

"Several hours ago he was shot about to commit a murder."

Just then the Sheriff's deputies moved in the direction of the Captain and his partner in training, they left quickly leaving Alex and Rupert unharmed.

Alex called Warren. "Rupert and I were cornered by the Captain and his partner, they were about to take me, I'm sure it was a one-way trip.

Rupert documented this on film. We have only enough to indict on threats against an undercover officer and robbery . . . he knows about Luke."

"No matter," Warren said, "he'll be coming after me, glad you're ok."

"Dawson and I will pursue, deputies follow us ASAP. More than likely he's headed for the morgue at County General."

"He'll try to kill you."

"I know. Get back to the shelter, if Rupert tries to follow, sit on him."

"Moseley has friends," Alex said.

Warren didn't answer as he pursued Moseley and his police protégé. The second car with Warren's men was about two miles behind following. Suddenly on the dark road a car pursuing them shot out two tires.

"Can't pursue," they said in a transmission to Warren, "they definitely only wanted to stop us."

"Understood," Dawson said. "I'm going to take the back seat and the shotgun."

Warren understood.

Captain Moseley was going in the direction of the hospital. When he arrived he knew Warren's men had been stopped which left only Dawson and Warren to deal with. He went to the morgue and saw the body of his son. Tears welled up in his eyes as he identified the body. His young partner could only stand by and watch.

"I want to know who shot him."

"Wouldn't the order have come from the Sheriff?"

"Yes, even if he didn't fire the shot."

"I'm going to kill him, let's go, I know he is coming here."

The second car of those loyal to Moseley then went after the Sheriff and Dawson. They pulled up alongside their SUV and began firing at the car. Dawson took the shotgun and positioned himself to fire at the pursuing car, he repeatedly did so as they fired. Then Warren heard a groan.

"I'm hit."

"How bad?"

"The shoulder . . . this is one dusty, dark stretch of road."

"Can you get yourself seated in front again?"

"I don't know, I'll aim for their tires if I don't pass out."

Warren heard three shots as Dawson kept firing, just then the pursuing car made a screeching sound and rolled several times.

"Dawson? Dawson?"

"I'm still here," he said sounding weak.

"Good shot . . . hang on, we're almost there."

"I'll try."

They arrived at the hospital, Dawson was taken by a trauma team. Warren's men in the second car contacted him, "Help is here, we're coming."

"Dawson is in the operating room, I'll stay until you arrive. Captain Moseley is probably still here."

Once Warren's men arrived one was stationed outside the operating room. He and the other looked for Captain Moseley and his partner.

"His police car is still here, the coroner met with him an hour ago as he identified his son, let's split up and find him."

From the Coroner's office to a parking building Warren searched. Then two voices were heard, Warren recognized one, he walked in that direction.

"You killed Luke," Captain Moseley said as he stepped out of the shadows.

They were standing facing each other. Warren didn't have time to defend himself. The Captain took his pistol.

"Luke and five thugs were about to kill a friend of mine, he was warned, he chose to ignore the warning, unfortunately he died, he admitted to having killed an undercover cop. You covered all his crimes and he kept harming and murdering innocent people."

Warren heard steps behind him, he saw Moseley's partner who asked, "Where is his deputy?"

"I haven't found him, the other one is stationed by the operating room, they're working on Dawson. No matter, we have the one I want."

"How many Bill? How many deaths?" Warren asked.

"I'm going to kill you, there isn't anyone waiting in the wings to help you, no T.V. cameras installed yet in this parking area."

"Your partner will be indicted for murder," Warren said feeling totally vulnerable and that he would die.

"I don't think he will, I won't. The best your agent Alex and the doctor with the camera got would be two overzealous cops trying to stop the flow of drugs into the homeless shelters and seizing money thought to be used for the sale of drugs."

Captain Moseley then drew his gun. Warren looked back at his partner who had a gun but still holstered, then Moseley shot Warren in the leg, he fell against a post, still standing trying to be brave he didn't cry out even with the intense pain.

"You will suffer."

"You molded Luke into everything you are."

Moseley then shot him again in the abdomen, Warren fell, he groaned in pain.

"I'm going to make you want to die. Do you know what it feels like to die?"

There was a pause as Warren looked into the face of evil then, "Yes, I know what it feels like to die and to be resurrected."

"Listen to this guy," Moseley said sarcastically to his partner, he then shot Warren in the shoulder. "After we're through with you we get Dawson."

"He had nothing to do with . . ."

"You gave the orders."

"He has a wife and child." Warren was about to pass out.

"Let's see where now? Were you planning to have children?"

Moseley is now standing over Warren preparing to fire, suddenly there is a shot, Captain Moseley falls beside Warren, his partner draws his gun as he turns to see Louie Lamour holding a gun.

"I'm crippled but I can still use a gun."

Warren quickly takes Moseley's gun and shoots his partner before he can finish off Louie who had dropped his gun. Louie moves toward Warren who is about to bleed out, he is shaking and is cold.

"Wipe your gun of prints, hide it someplace but hurry. Captain Moseley is dead," as he feels for a pulse, "his partner is dead I'm certain."

"Thanks Sheriff."

"I owe you Louie," barely able to speak now. Louie had already alerted security who had reports of gunfire, a trauma team then arrived. "How did you know where to find me Louie?" Warren asked.

"My secret." He follows as Warren is taken to the operating room. "Where is the deputy to protect you?"

"Still looking for me."

Dawson and Warren remained at the hospital several days. Louie stayed the night then was taken home to recover from the wounds inflicted by Luke. Giles and Max were told about the incident when Veronica called that first evening. They visited both Warren and Dawson insisting that one or both recuperate at the mansion. Warren did and Veronica stayed with him.

No one knew that Louie had shot Captain Moseley, Louie as instructed by Warren had wiped off the prints and hidden the gun. Warren cited that someone in the shadows had killed Moseley saving his life. While he recovered at the mansion he proposed marriage to Veronica who said "yes".

They married three weeks later at the mansion. Warren wore a black tuxedo. Louie was best man in a dark tuxedo with a lavender vest and fedora, Giles and Dawson wore similar tuxedos as groomsmen. Marilyn was matron of honor, Silvia and Nicole were bridesmaids and dressed in lavender, silk, knee length dresses. Veronica wore a white Vera Wang knee length silk dress with a small veil and entered to Spanish guitar music playing an Elton John favorite, "The Circle of Life." All took place at the mansion. It was a Baptist Ceremony, beautiful and uplifting, filled with goodwill for Veronica and Warren who had lived to marry his true love.

At the end, Warren made a tribute to the thirty peace officers representing the police and Sheriff's departments who were in attendance, he held back tears as he praised them for their service and sacrifice. "Now let's go down the hall and celebrate with Veronica and me." They did celebrate all night.

Rupert had made it home from the shelter after the danger passed three weeks earlier. He would get to know Matthew who was groomed and put to work. He wanted to meet Matthew's mother.

"The truth," Matthew said as he saw his mother's reaction to seeing Rupert. He kissed her and held her hand.

"Who are you Rupert?" Matthew asked.

Rupert sat by her still holding her hand, "I think I'm your father."

Matthew was stunned, he sat.

"Your ring, I gave one like it to Sarah twenty years ago. I tried to find her, she moved out of town, no contact, I didn't know she was pregnant."

Sarah spoke in a weak voice, "I didn't tell you."

Matthew was in disbelief at having a father and seeing his mother now able to speak a few words.

"I'm sorry Matthew," Rupert said.

Matthew looks at both his parents, "It should have been like this, always like this, a family . . . where do we go from here?"

"Take it one day at a time," Rupert told him.

Matthew had been in turmoil for years and now had a family.

-TO BE CONTINUED-

XX

Terms

STEM CELLS: Relatively undifferentiated cells of the lineage (family type) that retain the ability to divide and cycle throughout postnatal life to provide cells that can become specialized and take the place of those that die or are lost. Embryonic cells that can develop into different tissues. Stem cells are used in medical research. They differ from other types of cells in that they are unspecialized cells that can reproduce themselves for long periods of time using cell division but are capable of changing themselves into almost any type of specialist cell given the correct stimulus. Examples are cells that operate in the beating of the heart and cells in the pancreas.

EUKARYOTIC CELL: Cells of higher organisms, containing a true nucleus bounded by a nuclear membrane.

PROKARYOTIC CELL: Cells, such as those of bacteria and algae which lack a nuclear membrane so that the nuclear material is either scattered in the cytoplasm or collected in a nucleoid region.

REGENERATIVE RESEARCH: Where it concerns using stem cells to regenerate body parts as missing limbs, spinal cords and heart valves.

GENE: Specific sequences of nucleotides along a molecule of DNA (or, in the case of some viruses, RNA) which represent the functional units of heredity. Each person has 21,000 genes.

CORONER: Physicians appointed to investigate all cases of sudden or violent death.

MEDICAL EXAMINER: Physicians appointed to investigate all cases of sudden or violent death.

RNA: A polynucleotide consisting essentially of chains with a repeating backbone of phosphate and ribose units to which nitrogenous bases are attached. RNA is a biological macromolecule in that it can encode genetic information and serve as a structural component of cells. Stands for ribonucleic acid.

ANGIOGENESIS: Formation of new blood vessels.

FORENSICS: Scientific methods for solving crimes. The use of science or technology in the investigation and establishment of facts and evidence in a court of law.

FORENSIC PATHOLOGY: Branch of science that uses medical knowledge for legal purposes. Forensic pathology provides evidence that convicts the murderer.

PATHOLOGY: The branch of medicine dealing with the essential nature of disease especially changes in body tissues and organs caused by disease including postmortem.

CHROMOSOMES: In a prokaryotic cell or in the nucleus of a eukaryotic cell, a structure consisting of or containing DNA which carries the genetic information essential to the cell.

TELOMERES: A terminal section of a chromosome which has a specialized structure and is involved in chromosomal replication and stability. It's length is believed to be a few hundred base pairs. The tips of the chromosomes.

EPIGENOME: Sits atop the DNA and plays an active part in directing genes to behave in certain ways, by activating or silencing a gene.

Epigenetics is the science of studying epigenetic markers to predict and treat certain conditions.

DNA: A nucleic acid that carries the genetic information in the cell and is capable of self-replication and synthesis of RNA. DNA consists of two long chains of nucleotides twisted into a double helix and joined by hydrogen bonds between the complimentary bases adenine and thymine or cytosine and guanine. The sequence of nucleotides determines individual hereditary characteristics. DNA is the primary genetic material of all cells. Stands for Deoxyribonucleic acid.